CU01096057

I have edited Clive Gilson's books for
prolific and can turn his hand to many
contemporary novels, folklore and s
common theme is that none of them ever fails to take my breath
away. There's something in each story that is either memorably
poignant, hauntingly unnerving or sidesplittingly funny.

Lorna Howarth, *The Write Factor*

Tales From The World's Firesides is a grand project. I've collected
'000's of traditional texts as part of other projects, and while many
of the original texts are available through channels like Project
Gutenberg, some of the narratives can be hard to read by modern
readers, & so the Fireside project was born. Put simply, I collect,
collate & adapt traditional tales from around the world & publish
them for free as a modern archive. *Part 1* covers a host of nations
& regions across Europe. I'm not laying any claim to insight or
specialist knowledge, but these collections are born out of my love
of story-telling & I hope that you'll share my affection for
traditional tales, myths & legends.

Image by kalhh from Pixabay

ALSO BY CLIVE GILSON - *FICTION*

- Songs of Bliss
- Out of the walled Garden
- The Mechanic's Curse
- The Insomniac Booth
- A Solitude of Stars

AS EDITOR – *FIRESIDE TALES – Part 1, Europe*

- Tales from the Land of Dragons
- Tales from the Land of the Brave
- Tales from the Land of Saints and Scholars
- Tales from the Land of Hope and Glory
- Tales from Lands of Snow and Ice
- Tales from the Viking Isles
- Tales from the Forest Lands
- Tales from the Old Norse
- More Tales About Saints and Scholars
- More Tales About Hope and Glory
- More Tales About Snow and Ice
- Tales from the Land of Rabbits
- Tales Told by Bulls and Wolves
- Tales of Fire & Bronze
- Tales Told by the Samodivi
- Tales From The Land Of The Strigoi
- Tales Told By The Wind Mother
- Tales From Gallia
- Tales From Germania

EDITOR – *FIRESIDE TALES – Part 2, North America*

- Okaraxta - Tales from the Great Plains
- Tibik-kìzis – Tales from the Great Lakes & Canada

Further North American & Native American collections will be published during late 2019 & 2020

Tales from the Land of Dragons

Traditional tales, fables and sagas from Wales, a Celtic heartland...

Compiled, Adapted & Edited by Clive Gilson

Tales from the World's Firesides

Book 1 in Part 1 of the series: Europe

Tales From The Land Of Dragons, edited by Clive Gilson,
Solitude, Bath, UK

www.boyonabench.com

First published as an eBook in 2018

This edition © 2019 Clive Gilson

All rights reserved. No portion of this book may be reproduced in any form without permission from the publisher, except as permitted by United Kingdom copyright law.

This is a work of fiction. Names, characters, places, and incidents either are the products of the author's imagination or are used fictitiously. Any resemblance to actual persons, living or dead, businesses, companies, events, or locales is entirely coincidental.

Printed by IngramSpark

ISBN: 978-1-913500-04-7

SOLITUDE

CONTENTS

PREFACE

I've been collecting and telling stories for many years now, having had a number of my own works published in recent years, particularly focused on short story writing in the realms of magical realities and science fiction fantasies.

I've always drawn heavily on traditional folk and fairy tales, and in so doing have amassed a collection of many thousands of these tales from around the world. It has always been a long-standing intention to gather these stories together and to create a library of tales that tell the stories of places and peoples around the world.

Now that I've got a digitised archive up and running, I'm finally in a position to start on the great project... and this volume, *Tales from the Land of Dragons*, is the first in a set of collections covering the whole of the British Isles.

Time and facility allowing, I fully intend to go northwards next, covering the lands of ice and snow, before then heading south and east across Europe. Even then we'll just be scratching the surface. Far flung continents, lands and peoples beckon us ever onwards in our journey.

That's the great gift in storytelling. Since the first of our ancestors sat around in a cave somewhere, contemplating an ape's place in the world, we have, as a species, told each other stories of magic and cunning and caution and love. When I began to read through tales from the Celts, tales from Indonesia, tales from Africa and the

Far East, tales from everywhere, one of the things that struck me clearly was just how similar are the roots.

We share characters and characteristics. The natures of these tales are so similar underneath the local camouflage. We clearly share a storytelling heritage so much deeper than the world that we see superficially as always having been just as it is now.

These tales, whenever and wherever their origin, were originally told by firelight as a way of preserving histories and educating both adult and child. These tales form part of our shared heritage, witches, warts and all. They can be dark and violent. They can be sweet and loving. They are we and we are they in many, many ways.

Every story does, by the way, have a brief attribution, both of the original collector / writer and the title that this particular version has been adapted from. I've loved reading and re-reading all of these stories. I hope you do too.

Clive

Bath, 2018

A BOY THAT VISITED FAIRYLAND

Adapted from Welsh Fairy Tales by William Elliot Griffis and originally published in 1921.

MANY ARE THE PLACES IN WALES where the ground is lumpy and humpy with tumuli, or little artificial mounds. Among these the sheep graze, the donkeys bray, and the cows chew the cud. Here the ground is strewn with the ruins of cromlechs, or Cymric strongholds, of old Roman camps, of chapels and monasteries, showing that many different races of men have come and gone, while the birds still fly and the flowers bloom.

Centuries ago, the good monks of St. David had a school where lads were taught Latin and good manners. One of their pupils was a boy named Elidyr. He was such a poor scholar and he so hated books and loved play, that in his case spankings and whippings were almost of daily occurrence. Still he made no improvement. He was in the habit also of playing truant, or what one of the monks called "traveling to Baghdad." One of the consequences was that certain soft parts of his body, apparently provided by nature for this express purpose, often received a warming from his daddy.

His mother loved her boy dearly, and she often gently chided him, but he would not listen to her, and when she urged him to be more diligent, he ran out of the room. The monks did not spare the birch rod, and soon it was a case of a whipping for every lesson not learned.

One day, though he was only twelve years old, the boy started on a long run into the country. The further he got, the happier he felt, at least for one day. At night, tired out, he crept into a cave. When he woke up, in the morning, he thought it was glorious to be as free as the wild asses. So, like them, he quenched his thirst at the brook. But when, towards noon, he could find nothing to eat, and his inside cavity seemed to enlarge with very emptiness, his hunger grew every minute. Then he thought that a bit of oat cake, a leek, or a bowl of oatmeal, whether porridge or flummery, might suit a king.

He dared not go out far and pick berries, for, by this time, he saw that people were out searching for him. He did not feel yet, like going back to books, rods and scoldings, but the day seemed as long as a week. Meanwhile, he discovered that he had a stomach, which seemed to grow more and more into an aching void. He was glad when the sunset and darkness came. His bed was no softer in the cave, as he lay down with a stone for his pillow. Yet he had no dreams like those of Jacob and the angels.

When daylight came, the question in his mind was still, whether to stay and starve, or to go home and get two thrashings, one from his daddy, and another from the monks. But how about that thing inside of him, which seemed to be a live creature gnawing away, and which only something to eat would quiet? Finally, he came to a stern resolve. He started out, ready to face two whippings, rather than one death by starvation.

But he did not have to go home yet, for at the cave's mouth, he met two elves, who delivered a most welcome message. "Come with us to a land full of fun, play, and good things to eat."

All at once, his hunger left him, and he forgot that he ever wanted to swallow anything. All fear, or desire to go home, or to risk either schooling or a thrashing, passed away also. Into a dark passage all three went, but they soon came out into a beautiful country. How the birds sang, and the flowers bloomed! All around could be heard the joyful shouts of little folks at play. Never did things look so lovely.

Soon, in front of the broad path along which they were traveling, there rose up before him a glorious palace. It had a splendid gateway, and the silver-topped towers seemed to touch the blue sky. "What building is this?" asked the lad of his two guides.

They made answer that it was the palace of the King of Fairyland. Then they led him into the throne room, where, sat in golden splendour, a king, of august figure and of majestic presence, who was clad in resplendent robes. He was surrounded by courtiers in rich apparel, and all about him was magnificence, such as this boy, Elidyr, had never even read about or dreamed.

Yet everything was so small that it looked like Toy Land, and he felt like a giant among them, even though many of the little men around him were old enough to have whiskers on their cheeks and beards on their chins. The King spoke kindly to Elidyr, asking him who he was, and whence he had come.

While talking thus, the Prince, the King's only son appeared. He was dressed in white velvet and gold, and had a long feather in his cap. In the pleasantest way, he took Elidyr's hand and said, "Glad to see you. Come and let us play together."

That was just what Elidyr liked to hear. The King smiled and said to his visitor, "You will attend my son?" Then, with a wave of his hand, he signified to the boys to run out and play games, and a right merry time they did have, for there were many other little fellows for playmates.

These wee folks, with whom Elidyr played, were hardly as big as our babies, and certainly would not reach up to his mother's knee. To them, he looked like a giant, and he richly enjoyed the fun of having such little men, but with beards growing on their faces, look up to him. They played with golden balls, and rode little horses, with silver saddles and bridles, but these pretty animals were no larger than small dogs, or greyhounds.

No meat was ever seen on the table, but always plenty of milk. They never told a lie, nor used bad language, or swear-words. They often talked about mortal men, but usually to despise them; because what they liked to do, seemed so absurd and they always wanted foolish and useless things. To the elves, human beings were never satisfied, or long happy, even when they got what they wanted.

Everything in this part of fairyland was lovely, but it was always cloudy. No sun, star or moon was ever seen, yet the little men did not seem to mind it and enjoyed themselves every day. There was no end of play, and that suited Elidyr.

Yet by and by, he got tired even of games and play, and grew very homesick. He wanted to see his mother. So, he asked the King to let him visit his old home. He promised solemnly to come back, after a few hours. His Majesty gave his permission but charged him not to take with him anything whatever from fairyland, and to go with only the clothes on his back.

The same two elves or dwarfs, who had brought him into fairyland, were chosen to conduct him back. When they had led him again through the underground passage into the sunlight, they made him invisible until he arrived at his mother's cottage. She was overjoyed to find that no wolf had torn him to pieces, or wild bull had pushed him over a precipice. She asked him many questions, and he told her all he had seen, felt, or known.

When he rose up to go, she begged him to stay longer, but he said he must keep his word. Besides, he feared the rod of the monks, or his daddy, if he remained. So, he made his mother agree not to tell anything, not even to his father, as to where he was, or what he was doing. Then he made off and reported again to his playmates in fairyland.

The King was so pleased at the lad's promptness in returning, and keeping his word, and telling the truth, that he allowed him to go see his mother as often as he wanted to do so. He even gave orders releasing the two little men from constantly guarding him and told them to let the lad go alone, and when he would, for he always kept his word.

Many times did Elidyr visit his mother. By one road, or another, he made his way, keeping himself invisible all the time, until he got inside her cottage. He ran off, when anyone called in to pay a visit, or when he thought his daddy, or one of the monks was coming. He never saw any of these men.

One day, in telling his mother of the fun and good times he had in fairyland, he spoke of the heavy yellow balls, with which he and the King's sons played, and how these rolled around. Before leaving home, this boy had never seen any gold, and did not know what it was, but his mother guessed that it was the precious metal, of which the coins called sovereigns, and worth five dollars apiece, were made. So, she begged him to bring one of them back to her.

This, Elidyr thought, would not be right; but after much argument, his parents being poor, and she telling him that, out of hundreds in the King's palace, one single ball would not be missed, he decided to please her. So, one day, when he supposed no one was looking, he picked up one of the yellow balls and started off through the narrow dark passageway homeward. But no sooner was he back on the earth, and in the sunlight again, than he heard footsteps behind him. Then he knew that he had been discovered.

He glanced over his shoulder and there were the two little men, who had led him first and had formerly been his guards. They scowled at him as if they were mad enough to bite off the heads of tenpenny nails. Then they rushed after him, and there began a race to the cottage. But the boy had legs twice as long as the little men and got to the cottage door first. He now thought himself safe, but pushing open the door, he stumbled over the copper threshold, and the ball rolled out of his hand, across the floor of hardened clay, even to the nearly white-washed border, which ran about the edges of the room. It stopped at the feet of his mother, whose eyes opened wide at the sight of the ball of shining gold.

As he lay sprawling on the floor, and before he could pick himself up, one of the little men leaped over him, rushed into the room, and, from under his mother's petticoats, picked up the ball. They spat at the boy and shouted, "traitor," "rascal," "thief," "false mortal," "fox," "rat," "wolf," and other bad names. Then they turned and sped away.

Now Elidyr, though he had been a mischievous boy, often wilful, lazy, and never liking his books, had always loved the truth. He was very sad and miserable, beyond the telling, because he had broken his word of honour. So, almost mad with grief and shame, and from an accusing conscience, he went back to find the cave, in which he had slept. He would return to the King of the fairies, and ask his pardon, even if His Majesty never allowed him to visit Fairyland again.

But though he often searched and spent whole days in trying to find the opening in the hills, he could never discover it. So, fully penitent, and resolving to live right, and become what his father wanted him to be, he went back to the monastery.

There he plied his tasks so diligently that he excelled all in book-learning. In time, he became one of the most famous scholars in Welsh history. When he died, he asked to be buried, not in the monk's cemetery, but with his father and mother, in the churchyard. He made request that no name, record, or epitaph, be chiselled on his tomb, but only these words:

WE CAN DO NOTHING AGAINST THE TRUTH, BUT ONLY FOR THE TRUTH.

BETH GELLERT

Adapted from Celtic Fairy Tales by Joseph Jacobs, originally published in 1891.

IT WAS SOMEWHERE ABOUT 1200, AND Prince Llewellyn had a castle at Aber. Indeed, parts of the towers remain to this day. His consort was the Princess Joan; she was King John's daughter. Her coffin too remains with us to this day. Llewellyn was a great hunter of wolves and foxes, for the hills of Caernarvonshire were infested with wolves in those days, after the young lambs.

Prince Llewelyn had a favourite greyhound named Gellert that had been given to him by his father-in-law, King John. He was as gentle as a lamb at home but a lion in the chase. One day Llewelyn went to the chase and blew his horn in front of his castle. All his other dogs came to the call but Gellert never answered it. So, he blew a louder blast on his horn and called Gellert by name, but still the greyhound did not come. At last Prince Llewelyn could wait no longer and went off to the hunt without Gellert. He had little sport that day because Gellert was not there, the swiftest and boldest of his hounds.

He turned back in a rage to his castle, and as he came to the gate, who should he see but Gellert come bounding out to meet him. But when the hound came near him, the Prince was startled to see that his lips and fangs were dripping with blood. Llewelyn started back, and the greyhound crouched down at his feet as if surprised or afraid at the way his master greeted him.

Now Prince Llewelyn had a little son a year old with whom Gellert used to play, and a terrible thought crossed the Prince's mind that made him rush towards the child's nursery. And the nearer he came the more blood and disorder he found about the rooms. He rushed into it and found the child's cradle overturned and daubed with blood.

Prince Llewelyn grew more and more terrified and sought for his little son everywhere. He could find him nowhere but only signs of some terrible conflict in which much blood had been shed. At last he felt sure the dog had destroyed his child, and shouting to Gellert, "Monster, you have devoured my child," he drew out his sword and plunged it in the greyhound's side, who fell with a deep yell and still gazing in his master's eyes.

As Gellert raised his dying yell, a little child's cry answered it from beneath the cradle, and there Llewelyn found his child unharmed and just awakened from sleep. But just beside him lay the body of a great gaunt wolf all torn to pieces and covered with blood. Too late, Llewelyn learned what had happened while he was away. Gellert had stayed behind to guard the child and had fought and slain the wolf that had tried to destroy Llewelyn's heir.

In vain was all Llewelyn's grief; he could not bring his faithful dog to life again. "Oh, Gellert! Oh, Gellert!" said the prince, "my favourite hound, my favourite hound! You have been slain by your master's hand, and in death you have licked your master's hand!" He patted the dog, but it was too late, and poor Gellert died licking his master's hand.

Next day they made a coffin, and had a regular funeral, the same as if it were a human being; all the servants in deep mourning, and everybody. They made him a grave, and the village was called after the dog, Beth-Gellert, or Gellert's Grave; and the prince planted a tree, and put a gravestone of slate, though it was before the days of quarries. And they too are to be seen to this day.

BRYNEGLWYS WAGGONERS

Adapted from Welsh Folk-Lore by Owain Elias, published in 1896 by Woodall, Minshall and Co, and based on Elias' prize essay of the national Eisteddfod, 1887.

THE FOLLOWING TALE I RECEIVED FROM the mouth of Mr. Richard Jones, Ty'n-y-wern, Bryneglwys, near Corwen. Mr. Jones has stored up in his memory many tales of olden times, and he even thinks that he has himself seen a Fairy.

Standing by his farm, he pointed out to me on the opposite side of the valley a Fairy ring still green, where once, he said, the Fairies held their nightly revels. The scene of the tale which Mr. Jones related is wild, and a few years ago it was much more so than at present.

At the time that the event is said to have taken place the mountain was unenclosed, and there was not much travelling in those days, and consequently the Fairies could, undisturbed, enjoy their dances. But to proceed with the tale:

Two waggoners were sent from Bryneglwys for coals to the works over the hill beyond Minera. On their way they came upon a company of Fairies dancing with all their might. The men stopped to witness their movements, and the Fairies invited them to join in the dance.

One of the men stoutly refused to do so, but the other was induced to dance with the Fairies for a while. His companion looked on for a short time at the antics of his friend, and then shouted out that he would wait no longer, and desired the man to give up and come away. The dancing man, however, turned a deaf ear to the request, and no words could induce him to forego his dance. At last his companion said that he was going and requested his friend to follow him.

Taking the two waggons under his care he proceeded towards the coal pits, expecting every moment to be overtaken by his friend, but he was disappointed, for his friend never did appear.

The waggons and their loads were taken to Bryneglwys, and the man thought that perhaps his companion, having stopped too long in the dance, had turned homewards instead of following him to the coal pit. But on enquiry no one had heard or seen the missing waggoner.

One day the sensible waggoner met a Fairy on the mountain and inquired after his missing friend. The Fairy told him to go to a certain place, which he named, at a certain time, and that he should there see his friend. The man went, and there saw his companion just as he had left him, and the first words that he uttered were as follows; "Have the waggons gone far?"

The poor dancing waggoner never dreamt that months and months had passed away since he and his sensible companion had started out together to collect coal.

CADER IDRIS DANCERS

Adapted from British Goblins - Welsh Folk-lore, Fairy Mythology, Legends and Traditions by Wirt Sikes, United States Consul for Wales. Published by Sampson Low, Marston, Searle & Rivington in 1880

A COMPANY OF FAIRIES, WHICH FREQUENTED Cader Idris, were in the habit of going about from cottage to cottage in that part of Wales, in pursuit of information concerning the degree of benevolence possessed by the cottagers. Those who gave these fairies an ungracious welcome were subject to bad luck during the rest of their lives, but those who were good to the little folk became the recipients of their favour.

Old Morgan ap Rhys sat one night in his own chimney corner making himself comfortable with his pipe and his pint of cwrw da (good ale). The good ale having melted his soul a trifle, he was in a jollier mood than was natural to him, when there came a little rap at the door, which reached his ear dully through the smoke of his pipe and the noise of his own voice - for in his merriment Morgan was singing a roistering song, though he could not sing any better than a haw - which is Welsh for a donkey.

But Morgan did not take the trouble to get up at sound of the rap; his manners were not the most refined; he thought it was quite enough for a man bent on hospitality to bawl forth in ringing Welsh, "Gwaed dyn a'i gilydd! Why don't you come in when you've got as far as the door?" The welcome was not very polite, but it was sufficient. The door opened, and three travellers entered, looking worn and weary. Now these were the fairies from Cader Idris, disguised in this manner for purposes of observation, and Morgan never suspected they were other than they appeared.

"Good sir," said one of the travellers, "we are worn and weary, but all we seek is a bite of food to put in our wallet, and then we will go on our way."

"Ah, lads! Is that all you want? Well, there, look you, is the loaf and the cheese, and the knife lies by them, and you may cut what you like, and fill your bellies as well as your wallet, for never shall it be said that Morgan ap Rhys denied bread and cheese to a fellow creature."

The travellers proceeded to help themselves, while Morgan continued to drink and smoke, and to sing after his fashion, which was a very rough fashion indeed. As they were about to go, the fairy travellers turned to Morgan and said, "Since you have been so generous we will show that we are grateful. It is in our power to grant you any one wish you may have; therefore, tell us what that wish may be."

"Ho, ho!" said Morgan, 'Is that the case? Ah, I see you are making sport of me. Well, well, the wish of my heart is to have a harp that will play under my fingers no matter how ill I strike it; a harp that will play lively tunes, look you; no melancholy music for me!"

He had hardly spoken, when to his astonishment, there on the hearth before him stood a splendid harp, and he was suddenly alone. "Ah!" cried Morgan, "They're gone already." Then looking behind him he saw they had not taken the bread and cheese they had cut off, after all.

"Twas the fairies, perhaps," he muttered, but sat serenely quaffing his beer, and staring at the harp. There was a sound of footsteps behind him, and his wife came in from outdoors with some friends. Morgan feeling very jolly, thought he would raise a little laughter among them by displaying his want of skill upon the harp. So, he commenced to play, and oh, what a mad and capering tune it was!

"Well!" said Morgan, "but this is a strange harp. Hey, my friends, what ails you all?"

For as fast as he played his neighbours danced, every man, woman, and child of them all, footing it like mad creatures. Some of them bounded up against the roof of the cottage till their heads cracked again; others spun round and round, knocking over the furniture; and, as Morgan went on thoughtlessly playing, they began to pray to him to stop before they should be jolted to pieces. But Morgan found the scene too amusing to want to stop; besides, he was enamoured of his own suddenly developed skill as a musician; and he twanged the strings and laughed till his sides ached and the tears rolled down his cheeks, at the antics of his friends.

Tired out at last he stopped, and the dancers fell exhausted on the floor, the chairs, and the tables, declaring the devil himself was in the harp. "I know a tune worth two of that," said Morgan, picking up the harp again; but at sight of this motion all the company rushed from the house and escaped, leaving Morgan rolling merrily in his chair.

Whenever Morgan got a little tipsy after that, he would get the harp and set everybody round him to dancing; and the consequence was that he got a bad name, and no one would go near him. But all their precautions did not prevent the neighbours from being caught now and then, when Morgan took his revenge by making them dance till their legs were broken, or some other damage was done them.

Even lame people and invalids were compelled to dance whenever they heard the music of this diabolical telyn. In short, Morgan so abused his fairy gift that one night the good people came and took it away from him, and he never saw it more. The consequence was he became morose, and drank himself to death, which is a warning to all who accept from the fairies favours they do not deserve.

CROWS

Adapted from Fairy-Tales & Other Stories by Peter Henry Emerson,
published by D. Nutt, London in 1894.

ONE BLACK CROW, BAD LUCK FOR ME.

Two black crows, good luck for me.

Three black crows, a son shall be born in the family.

Four black crows, a daughter shall be born in the family.

Five black crows shall be a funeral in the family.

Six black crows, if they fly head on, a sudden death.

Seven black crows with their tails towards you, death within seven years.

There was a young man, not so very long ago, who had been to sea for years. He was married but had no children. He was one of the most spirited men you ever saw. He used to complain of his dreams.

He said, "All at once last Sunday I was up in the air, and I saw the vessel I was in going at great speed, making for a mountain, and I tried as hard as I could to keep her from the mountain. I don't believe I was asleep at all, I could see it so plainly. I went along in the air, looking at seven black crows all the time. I got dizzy, and the vessel seemed to lower on to the earth.

The vessel lowered within a few hundred feet of the earth, and I saw what I thought were fairies. I thought I had been there for days; in truth, it seemed to me I had been up there for three days, and that I could hear the fairies with mournful sounds drawing a coffin. I watched and watched and saw seven crows on the coffin. It seemed as if they were going to bury someone.

Whilst the coffin was going the seven crows flew up and bursted, and the heavens were illuminated more strongly than by the sun. Then I lost sight of the fairies, but saw some big giants in white walking about, and there was a big throne with a roof to it. And all at once I was in total darkness, but I could hear things flapping about, flying through the air.

Then I saw the moon rising and all the stars, and all sorts of objects flying through the air. And one came to me, and put his hand upon my shoulder, saying: 'Prepare to meet us tomorrow.' After that everything went dark again.

The first thing I knew I was in a ship steering, and the seven black crows were in front of me. I had a great trouble to steer my vessel. And as I went on the vessel struck a steeple, and exploded, and I awoke. Whereupon I jumped out of bed, looking very pale."

I left him on the beach late that morning, after he told me this, and he went home. When he got home he could see seven black crows on the house. Other people could see the crows but could not count them. He saw them all perched head on. He went into the house, and said, "There is something in these crows, Jane; see them on the roof."

She cried out and ran out and looked but could not see the seven. After that he didn't seem to be himself, though there was nothing the matter with him. A week afterwards, I went out on the Sunday morning after breakfast, and there was a seat on the beach, and on it sat this man, Johnny, and another man.

"Why, Johnny, you look very pale," I said.

"Do I?" he said.

"Yes! indeed you do," I replied.

"Well, I don't know, I have had such dreams."

"What will they have been, then?" I asked.

"That I was in a full-rigged ship, with all sails set; I was all alone, but could see nothing, only seven black crows. I counted them, but my wife could see nothing, but she could hear something."

That same day, when he went home, he said to his wife:

"Ah, Jane, there is something coming over me," and he fell down dead.

DAFYDD FAWR

*Adapted from Welsh Folk-Lore by Owain Elias, published in 1896
by Woodall, Minshall and Co, and based on Elias' prize essay of
the national Eisteddfod, 1887.*

A REVEREND FRIEND'S MOTHER, WHEN A young unmarried woman, started one evening from a house called Tyddyn Heilyn, in Penrhyndeudraeth, to her home at Penrhyn Isaf, accompanied by their servant man, David Williams, who was called, on account of his great strength and stature, Dafydd Fawr, (Big David). Dafydd was carrying home on his back a flitch of bacon. The night was dark, but calm, and Dafydd walked somewhat in the rear of his young mistress, and she, thinking he was following, went straight home. But three hours passed before Dafydd appeared with the pork on his back.

Dafydd was interrogated as to the cause of his delay, and in answer said he had only been following on about three minutes behind his young mistress. He was then told that she had arrived three hours before him, but this Dafydd would not believe. At length, however, he was convinced that he was wrong in his time-keeping, and then he proceeded to account for his lagging behind as follows:

Dafydd observed, he said, a brilliant meteor passing through the air, which was followed by a ring or hoop of fire, and within this hoop stood a man and woman of small size and handsomely dressed. With one arm they embraced each other, and with the other they took hold of the hoop, and their feet rested on the concave surface of the ring. When the hoop reached the earth these two beings jumped out of it, and immediately proceeded to make a circle on the ground.

As soon as this was done, a large number of men and women instantly appeared, and to the sweetest music that ear ever heard commenced dancing round and round the circle. The sight was so entrancing that Dafydd stayed for what he thought was just a few minutes to witness the scene. The ground all around was lit up by a kind of subdued light, and he observed every movement of these beings.

By and by the meteor which had at first attracted his attention appeared again, and then the fiery hoop came to view, and when it reached the spot where the dancing was, the lady and gentleman who had arrived in it jumped into the hoop and disappeared in the same manner in which they had reached the place. Immediately after their departure the Fairies vanished from sight, and Dafydd found himself alone and in darkness. Then he proceeded homewards, and in this way, he accounted for his delay on the way.

To this day it is still said that Glasynys still sings of the Fairy dancers:

The Fairy Tribe in merry crowds,

Under Dwynwen's calm protection,

Are seen in shady retreats

Chanting sweet melodies,

And spreading over the bushes

And the leafy groves

Illusion and phantasy on all that is green,

And whispering their mystic lore.

DICK THE FIDDLER AND THE FAIRY CROWN-PIECE

Adapted from Welsh Folk-Lore by Owain Elias, published in 1896 by Woodall, Minshall and Co, and based on Elias' prize essay of the national Eisteddfod, 1887.

DICK THE FIDDLER WAS IN THE habit of going about the country to play at merry-makings, fairs, and other public events. This worthy, after a week's fuddle at Darowen, wending his way homeward, had to walk down 'Fairy Green Lane,' just above the farmstead of Cefn Cloddiau. To banish fear, which he felt was gradually obtaining the mastery over him, and instead of just whistling, he drew out from the skirt pocket of his long-tailed great coat his favourite instrument. After tuning it, he commenced elbowing his way through his favourite air, Aden Ddu'r Fran (Crow's Black Wing).

When he passed over the green sward where the Tylwyth Têg, or Fairies, held their merry meetings, he heard something rattle in his fiddle, and this something continued rattling and tinkling until he reached Llwybr Scriw Riw, his home. By then he was almost out of his senses at the fright caused by that everlasting 'tink, rink, jink,' which was ever sounding in his ears.

Having entered the cottage he soon heard music of a different kind, in the harsh angry voice of his better half, who justly incensed at his absence, began lecturing him in a style, which, unfortunately, Dick, from habit, could not wholly appreciate. He was called a worthless fool, a regular drunkard and idler.

"How is it possible for me to beg enough for myself and half a house-full of children nearly naked, while you go about the country and bring me nothing home."

'Hush, hush, my good woman," said Dick, "see what's in the blessed old fiddle."

She obeyed, shook it, and out tumbled, to great surprise, a five-shilling piece. The wife looked up into the husband's face, saw that it was 'as pale as a sheet' with fright: and also noting that he had such an unusually large sum in his possession, she came to the conclusion that he could not live long, and accordingly changed her style saying, "Good man go to Llanidloes tomorrow, it is market-day and buy some shirting for yourself, for it may never be your good fortune to have such a sum of money again."

The following day, according to his wife's wishes, Dick wended his way to Llanidloes, musing, as he went along, upon his extraordinary luck, and unable to account for it. Arrived in the town, he entered Richard Evans's shop, and called for shirting linen to the value of five shillings, for which he gave the shopkeeper the crown piece taken out of the fiddle. Mr. Evans placed it in the till, and our worthy Dick betook himself to Betty Brunt's public-house in high glee with the capital piece of linen in the skirt pocket of his long-tailed top coat.

He had not, however, been long seated before Mr. Evans came in, and made sharp enquiries as to how and where he obtained possession of the crown piece with which he had paid for the linen. Dick assumed a solemn look, and then briefly related where and how he had received the coin.

"Say you so," said Evans, "I thought as much, for when I looked into the till, shortly after you left the shop, to my great surprise it was changed into a heap of musty horse dung."

ELIDORUS AND THE FAIRIES

Adapted from Welsh Folk-Lore by Owain Elias, published in 1896 by Woodall, Minshall and Co, and based on Elias' prize essay of the national Eisteddfod, 1887.

A SHORT TIME BEFORE OUR DAYS, a circumstance worthy of note occurred in these parts, which Elidorus, a priest, most strenuously affirmed had befallen to himself.

When a youth of twelve years, and learning his letters, since, as Solomon says, 'The root of learning is bitter, although the fruit is sweet,' in order to avoid the discipline and frequent stripes inflicted on him by his preceptor, he ran away and concealed himself under the hollow bank of the river.

After fasting in that situation for two days, two little men of pigmy stature appeared to him, saying, "If you will come with us, we will lead you into a country full of delights and sports."

Assenting and rising up, he followed his guides through a path, at first subterraneous and dark, into a most beautiful country, adorned with rivers and meadows, woods and plains, but obscure, and not illuminated with the full light of the sun. All the days were cloudy, and the nights extremely dark, on account of the absence of the moon and stars.

The boy was brought before the King and introduced to him in the presence of the court; who, having examined him for a long time, delivered him to his own son, who was then also still a boy. These men were of the smallest stature, but very well proportioned in their make; they were all of a fair complexion, with luxuriant hair falling over their shoulders like that of women. They had horses and greyhounds adapted to their size. They neither ate flesh nor fish, but lived on milk diet, made up into messes with saffron. They never took an oath, for they detested nothing so much as lies. As often as they returned from our upper hemisphere, they reprobated our ambition, infidelities, and inconstancies; they had no form of public worship, being strict lovers and reverers, as it seemed, of truth.

The boy in question frequently returned to our hemisphere, sometimes by the way he had first gone, sometimes by another; at first in company with other persons, and afterwards alone, and made himself known only to his mother, declaring to her the manners, nature, and state of the people he now lived with.

Being desired by her to bring a present of gold, with which that region abounded, he stole, while at play with the king's son, the golden ball with which he used to divert himself and brought it to his mother in great haste. When he reached the door of his father's house and was entering it in a great hurry as he was being pursued, his foot stumbled on the threshold and the boy fell down into the room where his mother was sitting. At that moment the two fairies appeared and seized the ball which had dropped from his hand and departed, showing the boy every mark of contempt and derision.

On recovering from his fall, confounded with shame, and execrating the evil counsel of his mother, he returned by the usual track to the subterraneous road, but found no appearance of any passage, though he searched for it on the banks of the river for nearly the space of a year. But since those calamities are often alleviated by time, which reason cannot mitigate, and length of time alone blunts the edge of our afflictions and puts an end to many evils, the youth, having been brought back by his friends and mother, and restored to his right way of thinking, and to his learning, in process of time attained the rank of priesthood.

Whenever David, Bishop of St. David's, talked to him in his advanced state of life concerning this event, the one-time fairy boy could never relate the particulars without shedding tears. He had made himself acquainted with the language of that nation, the words of which, in his younger days, he used to recite, which the bishop considered very similar to the Greek idiom.

When they asked for water, they said "Ydor ydorum," which meant "Bring water," for Ydor in their language, as well as in the Greek, signifies water, whence vessels for water are called Ãdriai. Dwr, also in the British language, signifies water. When they wanted salt they said "Halgein ydorum," "Bring salt." Salt is called al in Greek, and Halen in old British, because the Britons (then called Trojans and afterwards Britons, from Brito, their leader) remained in Greece after the destruction of Troy, and so became, in many instances, similar to the Greek.

FFRIDD YR YWEN

*Adapted from Welsh Folk-Lore by Owain Elias, published in 1896
by Woodall, Minshall and Co, and based on Elias' prize essay of
the national Eisteddfod, 1887.*

IN MATHAVARN, IN THE PARISH OF Llanwrin, and the
Cantrev of Cyveilioc, there is a wood which is called Ffridd yr
Ywen (Forest of the Yew); it is supposed to be so called because
there is a yew tree growing in the very middle of it. In many parts
of the wood are to be seen green circles, which are called 'the
dancing places of the goblins,' about which, a considerable time
ago, the following tale was very common in the neighbourhood.

Two servants of John Pugh, Esq., went out one day to work in the
Ffridd yr Ywen. Pretty early in the afternoon the whole country
was so covered with dark vapour, that the youths thought night was
coming on; but when they came to the middle of the 'Forest' it
brightened up around them and the darkness seemed all left behind;
so, thinking it too early to return home for the night, they lay down
and slept.

One of them, on waking, was much surprised to find no one there
but himself; he wondered a good deal at the behaviour of his
companion but made up his mind at last that he had gone on some
business of his own, as he had been talking of it for some time

before; so, the sleeper went home, and when they inquired after his companion, he told them he was gone to the cobbler's shop. The next day they inquired of him again about his fellow-servant, but he could not give them any account of him; but at last confessed how and where they had both gone to sleep.

After searching and searching many days, the servant man went to a gwr cyvarwydd (a conjuror), which was a very common trade in those days, according to the legend; and the conjuror said to him, "Go to the same place where you and the lad slept; go there exactly a year after the boy was lost; let it be on the same day of the year, and at the same time of the day, but take care that you do not step inside the Fairy ring, stand on the border of the green circles you saw there, and the boy will come out with many of the goblins to dance, and when you see him so near to you that you may take hold of him, snatch him out of the ring as quickly as you can."

He did according to this advice, and plucked the boy out, and then asked him, "if he did not feel hungry," to which his once lost companion answered "No," for he had still the remains of his dinner that he had left in his wallet before going to sleep, and he asked, "if it was not nearly night, and time to go home," not knowing that a year had passed by.

His look was like a skeleton, and, of course, as soon as he tasted food he was a dead man.

GWRGAN FARFDRWCH'S FABLE

Adapted from Fairy-Tales & Other Stories by Peter Henry Emerson,
published by D. Nutt, London in 1894.

HEAR ME, OH YE BRITONS! ON the top of a high rock in Arvon there stood a goat, which a lion perceiving from the valley below, addressed her in this manner:

"My dearest neighbour, why do you prefer that dry barren rock to feed on? Come down to this charming valley, where you mayest feed luxuriously upon all sorts of dainties, amongst flowers in shady groves, made fruitful by meandering brooks."

"I am much obliged to you, master," replied the goat; "perhaps you mean well, and tell me the truth, but you have very bad neighbours, whom I do not like to trust, and those are your teeth, so, with your leave, I prefer staying where I am."

HAVELOK THE DANE

Adapted from Hero-Myths & Legends of the British Race by Maud Isabel Ebbutt, published by George G. Harrap & Co in 1910.

Havelok and Godard

IN DENMARK, LONG AGO, LIVED A good king named Birkabeyn, rich and powerful, a great warrior and a man of mighty prowess, whose rule was undisputed over the whole realm. He had three children; two daughters, named Swanborow and Elfleda the Fair, and one young and goodly son, Havelok, the heir to all his dominions.

All too soon came the day that no man can avoid, when Death would call King Birkabeyn away, and he grieved sore over his young children to be left fatherless and unprotected; but, after much reflection, and prayers to God for wisdom to help his choice, he called to him Jarl Godard, a trusted counsellor and friend, and committed into his hands the care of the realm and of the three royal children, until Havelok should be of age to be knighted and rule the land himself. King Birkabeyn felt that such a charge was too great a temptation for any man unbound by oaths of fealty and honour, and although he did not distrust his friend, he required Godard to swear,

By altar and by holy service book,

By bells that call the faithful to the church,

By blessed sacrament, and sacred rites,

By Holy Rood, and Him who died thereon,

That you will truly rule and keep my realm,

Wilt guard my babes in love and loyalty,

Until my son be grown, and dubbèd knight:

That you will then resign to him his land,

His power and rule, and all that owns his sway.

Jarl Godard took this most solemn oath at once with many protestations of affection and whole-hearted devotion to the dying king and his heir, and King Birkabeyn died happy in the thought that his children would be well cared for during their helpless youth.

When the funeral rites were celebrated Jarl Godard assumed the rule of the country, and, under pretext of securing the safety of the royal children, removed them to a strong castle, where no man was allowed access to them, and where they were kept so closely that the royal residence became a prison in all but name. Godard, finding Denmark submit to his government without resistance, began to adopt measures to rid himself of the real heirs to the throne, and gave orders that food and clothes should be supplied to the three children in such scanty quantities that they might die of hardship; but since they were slow to succumb to this cruel, torturing form of murder, he resolved to slay them suddenly, knowing that no one durst call him to account. Having steeled his heart against all pitiful thoughts, he went to the castle, and was taken to the inner dungeon where the poor babes lay shivering and weeping for cold and hunger. As he entered, Havelok, who was even then a bold lad, greeted him courteously, and knelt before him, with clasped hands, begging a boon.

"Why do you weep and wail so sore?" asked Godard.

"Because we are so hungry," answered Havelok. "We have so little food, and we have no servants to wait on us; they do not give us half as much as we could eat; we are shivering with cold, and our clothes are all in rags. Woe to us that we were ever born! Is there in the land no more corn with which men can make bread for us? We are nearly dead from hunger."

These pathetic words had no effect on Godard, who had resolved to yield to no pity and show no mercy. He seized the two little girls as they lay cowering together, clasping one another for warmth, and cut their throats, letting the bodies of the hapless babies fall to the floor in a pool of blood; and then, turning to Havelok, aimed his knife at the boy's heart. The poor child, terrified by the awful fate of the two girls, knelt again before him and begged for mercy:

Fair lord, have mercy on me now, I pray!

Look on my helpless youth, and pity me!

Oh, let me live, and I will yield you all -

My realm of Denmark will I leave to you,

And swear that I will ne'er assail your sway.

Oh, pity me, lord! be compassionate!

And I will flee far from this land of mine,

And vow that Birkabeyn was ne'er my sire!

Jarl Godard was touched by Havelok's piteous speech, and felt some faint compassion, so that he could not slay the lad himself; yet he knew that his only safety was in Havelok's death.

"If I let him go," thought he, "Havelok will at last work me woe! I shall have no peace in my life, and my children after me will not hold the lordship of Denmark in safety, if Havelok escapes! Yet I cannot slay him with my own hands. I will have him cast into the sea with an anchor about his neck: thus at least his body will not float."

Godard left Havelok kneeling in terror, and, striding from the tower, leaving the door locked behind him, he sent for an ignorant fisherman, Grim, who, he thought, could be frightened into doing his will. When Grim came he was led into an ante-room, where Godard, with terrible look and voice, addressed him thus:

"Grim, you know you are my thrall." "Yea, fair lord," said Grim, trembling at Godard's stern voice. "And I can slay you if you dost disobey me." "Yea, lord; but how have I offended you?" "You have not yet; but I have a task for thee, and if you dost it not, dire punishment shall fall upon thee." "Lord, what is the work that I must do?" asked the poor fisherman. "Tarry: I will show thee." Then Godard went into the inner room of the tower, whence he returned leading a fair boy, who wept bitterly. "Take this boy secretly to your house and keep him there till dead of night; then launch your boat, row out to sea, and fling him therein with an anchor round his neck, so that I shall see him never again."

Grim looked curiously at the weeping boy, and said, "What reward shall I have if I work this sin for you?"

Godard replied: "The sin will be on my head as I am your lord and bid you do it; but I will make you a freeman, noble and rich, and my friend, if you will do this secretly and discreetly."

Thus reassured and bribed, Grim suddenly took the boy, flung him to the ground, and bound him hand and foot with cord which he took from his pockets. So anxious was he to secure the boy that he drew the cords very tight, and Havelok suffered terrible pain; he could not cry out, for a handful of rags was thrust into his mouth and over his nostrils, so that he could hardly breathe. Then Grim flung the poor boy into a horrible black sack, and carried him thus from the castle, as if he were bringing home broken food for his family. When Grim reached his poor cottage, where his wife Leve was waiting for him, he slung the sack from his shoulder and gave it to her, saying, "Take good care of this boy as of your life. I am to drown him at midnight, and if I do so my lord has promised to make me a free man and give me great wealth."

When Dame Leve heard this, she sprang up and flung the lad down in a corner, and nearly broke his head with the crash against the earthen floor. There Havelok lay, bruised and aching, while the couple went to sleep, leaving the room all dark but for the red glow from the fire. At midnight Grim awoke to do his lord's behest, and Dame Leve, going to the living-room to kindle a light, was terrified by a mysterious gleam as bright as day which shone around the boy on the floor and streamed from his mouth. Leve hastily called Grim to see this wonder, and together they released Havelok from the gag and bonds and examined his body, when they found on the right shoulder the token of true royalty, a cross of red gold.

"God knows," said Grim, "that this is the heir of our land. He will come to rule in good time, will bear sway over England and Denmark, and will punish the cruel Godard." Then, weeping sore, the loyal fisherman fell down at Havelok's feet, crying, "Lord, have mercy on me and my wife! We are your thralls, and never will we do aught against thee. We will nourish you until you can rule and will hide you from Godard; and you will perchance give me my freedom in return for your life."

At this unexpected address Havelok sat up surprised and rubbed his bruised head and said, "I am nearly dead, what with hunger, and your cruel bonds, and the gag. Now bring me food in plenty!" "Yea, lord," said Dame Leve, and bustled about, bringing the best they had in the hut; and Havelok ate as if he had fasted for three days; and then he was put to bed, and slept in peace while Grim watched over him.

However, Grim went the next morning to Jarl Godard and said, "Lord, I have done your behest, and drowned the boy with an anchor about his neck. He is safe, and now, I pray you, give me my reward, the gold and other treasures, and make me a freeman as you have promised." But Godard only looked fiercely at him and said, "What, would you be an earl? Go home, you foul churl, and be ever a thrall! It is enough reward that I do not hang you now for insolence, and for your wicked deeds. Go speedily, else you mayst stand and palter with me too long." And Grim shrank quietly away, lest Godard should slay him for the murder of Havelok.

Now Grim saw in what a terrible plight he stood, at the mercy of this cruel and treacherous man, and he took counsel with himself and consulted his wife, and the two decided to flee from Denmark to save their lives. Gradually Grim sold all his stock, his cattle, his nets, everything that he owned, and turned it into good pieces of gold; then he bought and secretly fitted out and provisioned a ship, and at last, when all was ready, carried on board Havelok (who had lain hidden all this time), his own three sons and two daughters;

then when he and his wife had gone on board he set sail, and, driven by a favourable wind, reached the shores of England.

Goldborough and Earl Godrich

Meanwhile in England a somewhat similar fate had befallen a fair princess named Goldborough. When her father, King Athelwold, lay dying all his people mourned, for he was the flower of all fair England for knighthood, justice, and mercy; and he himself grieved sorely for the sake of his little daughter, soon to be left an orphan. "What will she do?" moaned he. "She can neither speak nor walk! If she were only able to ride, to rule England, and to guard herself from shame, I should have no grief, even if I died and left her alone, while I lived in the joy of paradise!"

Then Athelwold summoned a council to be held at Winchester and asked the advice of the nobles as to the care of the infant Goldborough. They with one accord recommended Earl Godrich of Cornwall to be made regent for the little princess; and the earl, on being appointed, swore with all solemn rites that he would marry her at twelve years old to the highest, the best, fairest, and strongest man alive, and in the meantime would train her in all royal virtues and customs. So, King Athelwold died, and was buried with great lamentations, and Godrich ruled the land as regent. He was a strict but just governor, and England had great peace, without and within, under his severe rule, for all lived in awe of him, though no man loved him. Goldborough grew and throve in all ways and became famous through the land for her gracious beauty and gentle and virtuous demeanour. This roused the jealousy of Earl Godrich, who had played the part of king so long that he almost believed himself King of England, and he began to consider how he could secure the kingdom for himself and his son. Thereupon he had Goldborough taken from Winchester, where she kept royal state, to Dover, where she was imprisoned in the castle, and strictly secluded from all her friends; there she remained, with poor clothes and scanty food, awaiting a champion to uphold her right.

Havelok Becomes Cook's Boy

When Grim sailed from Denmark to England he landed in the Humber, at the place now called Grimsby, and there established himself as a fisherman. So successful was he that for twelve years he supported his family well, and carried his catches of fish far afield, even to Lincoln, where rare fish always brought a good price. In all this time Grim never once called on Havelok for help in the task of feeding the family; he reverenced his king, and the whole household served Havelok with the utmost deference, and often went with scanty rations to satisfy the boy's great appetite. At length Havelok began to think how selfishly he was living, and how much food he consumed, and was filled with shame when he realized how his foster-father toiled unweariedly while he did nothing to help. In his remorseful meditations it became clear to him that, though a king's son, he ought to do some useful work. "Of what use," thought he, "is my great strength and stature if I do not employ it for some good purpose? There is no shame in honest toil. I will work for my food, and try to make some return to Father Grim, who has done so much for me. I will gladly bear his baskets of fish to market, and I will begin tomorrow."

On the next day, in spite of Grim's protests Havelok carried a load of fish equal to four men's burden to Grimsby market, and sold it successfully, returning home with the money he received; and this he did day by day, till a famine arose and fish and food both became scarce. Then Grim, more concerned for Havelok than for his own children, called the youth to him and bade him try his fortunes in Lincoln, for his own sake and for theirs; he would be better fed, and the little food Grim could get would go further among the others if Havelok were not there. The one obstacle in the way was Havelok's lack of clothes, and Grim overcame that by sacrificing his boat's sail to make Havelok a coarse tunic. That done, they bade each other farewell, and Havelok started for Lincoln, barefooted and bareheaded, for his only garment was the sailcloth tunic. In Lincoln Havelok found no friends and no food for two days, and he was desperate and faint with hunger, when he heard a call: "Porters, porters! hither to me!" Roused to new vigour by the chance of work, Havelok rushed with the rest, and bore down and hurled aside the other porters so vigorously that he was chosen to carry provisions for Bertram, the earl's cook; and in return he received the first meal he had eaten for nearly three days.

On the next day Havelok again overthrew the porters, and, knocking down at least sixteen, secured the work. This time he had to carry fish, and his basket was so laden that he bore nearly a cartload, with which he ran to the castle. There the cook, amazed at his strength, first gave him a hearty meal, and then offered him good service under himself, with food and lodging for his wages. This offer Havelok accepted, and was installed as cook's boy, and employed in all the lowest offices - carrying wood, water, turf, hewing logs, lifting, fetching, carrying - and in all he showed himself a wonderfully strong worker, with unfailing good temper and gentleness, so that the little children all loved the big, gentle, fair-haired youth who worked so quietly and played with them so merrily. When Havelok's old tunic became worn out, his master, the cook, took pity on him and gave him a new suit, and then it could be seen how handsome and tall and strong a youth this cook's boy really was, and his fame spread far and wide round Lincoln Town.

Havelok and Goldborough

At the great fair of Lincoln, sports of all kinds were indulged in, and in these Havelok took his part, for the cook, proud of his mighty scullion, urged him to compete in all the games and races. As Earl Godrich had summoned his Parliament to meet that year at Lincoln, there was a great concourse of spectators, and even the powerful Earl Regent himself sometimes watched the sports and cheered the champions. The first contest was "putting the stone," and the stone chosen was so weighty that none but the most stalwart could lift it above the knee - none could raise it to his breast. This sport was new to Havelok, who had never seen it before, but when the cook bade him try his strength he lifted the stone easily and threw it more than twelve feet. This mighty deed caused his fame to be spread, not only among the poor servants with whom Havelok was classed, but also among the barons, their masters, and Havelok's Stone became a landmark in Lincoln. Thus, Godrich heard of a youth who stood head and shoulders taller than other men and was stronger, more handsome - and yet a mere common scullion. The news brought him a flash of inspiration: "Here is the highest, strongest, best man in all England, and him shall Goldborough wed. I shall keep my vow to the letter, and England must fall to me, for Goldborough's royal blood will be lost by her marriage with a thrall, the people will refuse her obedience, and England will cast her out."

Godrich therefore brought Goldborough to Lincoln, received her with bell-ringing and seemly rejoicing, and bade her prepare for her wedding. This the princess refused to do until she knew who her destined husband was, for she said she would wed no man who was not of royal birth. Her firmness drove Earl Godrich to fierce wrath, and he burst out: "Wilt you be queen and mistress over me? Your pride shall be brought down: you shall have no royal spouse: a vagabond and scullion shall you wed, and that no later than tomorrow! Curses on him who speaks you fair!" In vain the princess wept and bemoaned herself: the wedding was fixed for the morrow morn.

The next day at dawn Earl Godrich sent for Havelok, the mighty cook's boy, and asked him: "Wilt you take a wife?"

"Nay," said Havelok, "that will I not. I cannot feed her, much less clothe and lodge her. My very garments are not my own, but belong to the cook, my master." Godrich fell upon Havelok and beat him furiously, saying, "Unless you will take the wench I give you for wife I will hang or blind thee"; and so, in great fear, Havelok agreed to the wedding. At once Goldborough was brought, and forced into an immediate marriage, under penalty of banishment or burning as a witch if she refused. And thus, the unwilling couple were united by the Archbishop of York, who had come to attend the Parliament.

Never was there so sad a wedding! The people murmured greatly at this unequal union, and pitied the poor princess, thus driven to wed a man of low birth; and Goldborough herself wept pitifully but resigned herself to God's will. All men now acknowledged with grief that she and her husband could have no claim to the English throne, and thus Godrich seemed to have gained his object. Havelok and his unwilling bride recognised that they would not be safe near Godrich, and as Havelok had no home in Lincoln to which he could take the princess, he determined to go back to his faithful foster-father, Grim, and put the fair young bride under his loyal protection. Sorrowfully, with grief and shame in their hearts, Havelok and Goldborough made their way on foot to Grimsby, only to find the loyal Grim dead; but his five children were alive and in prosperity. When they saw Havelok and his wife they fell on their knees and saluted them with all respect and reverence. In their joy to see their king again, these worthy fisherfolk forgot their newly won wealth, and said, "Welcome, dear lord, and your fair lady! What joy is ours to see you again, for your subjects are we, and you can do with us as you wilt. All that we have is thine, and if you will dwell with us we will serve you and your wife truly in all ways!" This greeting surprised Goldborough, who began to suspect some mystery, and she was greatly comforted when brothers and sisters busied themselves in lighting fires, cooking meals, and waiting on her hand and foot, as if she had been indeed a king's wife. Havelok, however, said nothing to explain the mystery, and Goldborough that night lay awake bewailing her fate as a thrall's bride, even though he was the fairest man in England.

The Revelation and Return to Denmark

As Goldborough lay sleepless and unhappy she became aware of a brilliant light shining around Havelok and streaming from his mouth; and while she feared and wondered an angelic voice cried to her:

Fair Princess, cease this grief and heavy moan!

For Havelok, your newly wedded spouse,

Is son and heir to famous kings: the sign

You find in the cross of ruddy gold

That shines on his shoulder. He shall be

Monarch and ruler of two mighty realms;

Denmark and England shall obey his rule,

And he shall sway them with a sure command.

This shall you see with your own eyes, and be

Lady and Queen, with Havelok, o'er these lands.

This angelic message so gladdened Goldborough that she kissed, for the first time, her unconscious husband, who started up from his sleep, saying, "Dear love, are you sleeping? I have had a wondrous dream. I thought I sat on a lofty hill and saw all Denmark before me. As I stretched out my arms I embraced it all, and the people clung to my arms, and the castles fell at my feet; then I flew over the salt sea with the Danish people clinging to me, and I closed all fair England in my hand, and gave it to thee, dear love! Now what can this mean?"

Goldborough answered joyfully: "It means, dear heart, that you shall be King of Denmark and of England too: all these realms shall fall into your power, and you shall be ruler in Denmark within one year. Now do you follow my advice, and let us go to Denmark, taking with us Grim's three sons, who will accompany you for love and loyalty; and have no fear, for I know you will succeed."

The next morning Havelok went to church early and prayed humbly and heartily for success in his enterprise and retribution on the false traitor Godard; then, laying his offering on the altar before the Cross, he went away glad in heart. Grim's three sons, Robert the Red, William Wendut, and Hugh the Raven, joyfully consented to go with Havelok to Denmark, to attack with all their power the false Jarl Godard and to win the kingdom for the rightful heir. Their wives and families stayed in England, but Goldborough would not leave her husband, and after a short voyage the party landed safely on the shores of Denmark, in the lands of Jarl Ubbe, an old friend of King Birkabeyn, who lived far from the court now that a usurper held sway in Denmark.

Havelok and Ubbe

Havelok dared not reveal himself and his errand until he knew more of the state of parties in the country, and he therefore only begged permission to live and trade there, giving Ubbe, as a token of goodwill and a tribute to his power, a valuable ring, which the jarl prized greatly. Ubbe, gazing at the so-called merchant's great stature and beauty, lamented that he was not of noble birth, and planned to persuade him to take up the profession of arms. At first, however, he simply granted Havelok permission to trade, and invited him and Goldborough to a feast, promising them safety and honour under his protection. Havelok dreaded lest his wife's beauty might place them in jeopardy, but he dared not refuse the invitation, which was pointedly given to both; accordingly, when they went to Ubbe's hall, Goldborough was escorted by Robert the Red and William Wendut.

Ubbe received them with all honour, and all men marvelled at Goldborough's beauty, and Ubbe's wife loved Goldborough at first sight as her husband did Havelok, so that the feast passed off with all joy and mirth, and none dared raise a hand or lift his voice against the wandering merchant whom Ubbe so strangely favoured. But Ubbe knew that when once Havelok and his wife were away from his protection there would be little safety for them, since the rough Danish nobles would think nothing of stealing a trader's fair wife, and many a man had cast longing eyes on Goldborough's loveliness. Therefore, when the feast was over, and Havelok took his leave, Ubbe sent with him a body of ten knights and sixty men-at-arms, and recommended them to the magistrate of the town, Bernard Brown, a true and upright man, bidding him, as he prized his life, keep the strangers in safety and honour.

Well it was that Ubbe and Bernard Brown took these precautions, for late at night a riotous crowd came to Bernard's house clamouring for admittance. Bernard withstood the angry mob, armed with a great axe, but they burst the door in by hurling a huge stone; and then Havelok joined in the defence. He drew out the great beam which barred the door, and crying, "Come quickly to me, and you shall stay here! Curses on him who flees!" began to lay about him with the big beam, so that three fell dead at once. A terrible fight followed, in which Havelok, armed only with the beam, slew twenty men in armour, and was then sore beset by the rest of the troop, aiming darts and arrows at his unarmoured breast. It was going hardly with him, when Hugh the Raven, hearing and understanding the cries of the assailants, called his brothers to their lord's aid, and they all joined the fight so furiously that, long ere day, of the sixty men who had attacked the inn not one remained alive.

In the morning news was brought to Jarl Ubbe that his stranger guest had slain sixty of the best of his soldiery.

"What can this mean?" said Ubbe. "I had better go and see to it myself, for any messenger would surely treat Havelok discourteously, and I should be full loath to do that." He rode away to the house of Bernard Brown and asked the meaning of its damaged and battered appearance.

"My lord," answered Bernard Brown, "last night at moonrise there came a band of sixty thieves who would have plundered my house and bound me hand and foot. When Havelok and his companions saw it they came to my aid, with sticks and stones, and drove out the robbers like dogs from a mill. Havelok himself slew three at one blow. Never have I seen a warrior so good! He is worth a thousand in a fray. But alas! he is grievously wounded, with three deadly gashes in side and arm and thigh, and at least twenty smaller wounds. I am scarcely harmed at all, but I fear he will die full soon."

Ubbe could scarcely believe so strange a tale, but all the bystanders swore that Bernard told nothing but the bare truth, and that the whole gang of thieves, with their leader, Griffin the Welshman, had been slain by the hero and his small party. Then Ubbe bade them bring Havelok, that he might call a leech to heal his wounds, for if the stranger merchant should live Jarl Ubbe would without fail dub him knight; and when the leech had seen the wounds he said the patient would make a good and quick recovery. Then Ubbe offered Havelok and his wife a dwelling in his own castle, under his own protection, till Havelok's grievous wounds were healed. There, too, fair Goldborough would be under the care of Ubbe's wife, who would cherish her as her own daughter. This kind offer was accepted gladly, and they all went to the castle, where a room was given them next to Ubbe's own.

At midnight Ubbe woke, aroused by a bright light in Havelok's room, which was only separated from his own by a slight wooden partition. He was vexed suspecting his guest of midnight wassailing and went to inquire what villainy might be hatching. To his surprise, both husband and wife were sound asleep, but the light shone from Havelok's mouth, and made a glory round his head. Utterly amazed at the marvel, Ubbe went away silently, and returned with all the garrison of his castle to the room where his guests still lay sleeping. As they gazed on the light Havelok turned in his sleep, and they saw on his shoulder the golden cross, shining like the sun, which all men knew to be the token of royal birth. Then Ubbe exclaimed: "Now I know who this is, and why I loved him so dearly at first sight: this is the son of our dead King Birkabeyn. Never was man so like another as this man is to the dead king: he is his very image and his true heir." With great joy they fell on their knees and kissed him eagerly, and Havelok awoke and began to scowl furiously, for he thought it was some treacherous attack; but Ubbe soon undeceived him.

'Dear lord,' said he, 'be you in naught dismayed,

For in your eyes methinks I see your thought -

Dear son, great joy is mine to live this day!

My homage, lord, I freely offer thee:

Your loyal men and vassals are we all,

For you are son of mighty Birkabeyn,

And soon shall conquer all your father's land,

Though you are young and almost friendless here.

Tomorrow will we swear our fealty due,

And dub you knight, for prowess unexcelled.

Now Havelok knew that his worst danger was over, and he thanked God for the friend He had sent him and left to the good Jarl Ubbe the management of his cause. Ubbe gathered an assembly of as many mighty men of the realm, and barons, and good citizens, as he could summon; and when they were all assembled, pondering what was the cause of this imperative summons, Ubbe arose and said:

"Gentles, bear with me if I tell you first things well known to you. Ye know that King Birkabeyn ruled this land until his death-day, and that he left three children - one son, Havelok, and two daughters - to the guardianship of Jarl Godard: ye all heard him swear to keep them loyally and treat them well. But ye do not know how he kept his oath! The false traitor slew both the maidens, and would have slain the boy, but for pity he would not kill the child with his own hands. He bade a fisherman drown him in the sea; but when the good man knew that it was the rightful heir, he saved the boy's life and fled with him to England, where Havelok has been brought up for many years. And now, behold! here he stands. In all the world he has no peer, and ye may well rejoice in the beauty and manliness of your king. Come now and pay homage to Havelok, and I myself will be your leader!"

Jarl Ubbe turned to Havelok, where he stood with Goldborough beside him, and knelt before him to do homage, an example which was followed by all present. At a second and still larger assembly held a fortnight later a similar oath of fealty was sworn by all, Havelok was dubbed knight by the noble Ubbe, and a great festival was celebrated, with sports and amusements for the populace. A council of war and vengeance was held with the great nobles.

The Death of Godard

Havelok, now acknowledged King of Denmark, was unsatisfied until he had punished the treacherous Godard, and he took a solemn oath from his soldiers that they would never cease the search for the traitor till they had captured him and brought him bound to judgment. After all, Godard was captured as he was hunting. Grim's three sons, now knighted by King Havelok, met him in the forest, and bade him come to the king, who called on him to remember and account for his treatment of Birkabeyn's children. Godard struck out furiously with his fists, but Sir Robert the Red wounded him in the right arm. When Godard's men joined in the combat, Robert and his brothers soon slew ten of their adversaries, and the rest fled; returning, ashamed at the bitter reproaches of their lord, they were all slain by Havelok's men. Godard was taken, bound hand and foot, placed on a miserable jade with his face to the tail, and so led to Havelok. The king refused to be the judge of his own cause and entrusted to Ubbe the task of presiding at the traitor's trial. No mercy was shown to the cruel Jarl Godard, and he was condemned to a traitor's death, with torments of terrible barbarity. The sentence was carried out to the letter, and Denmark rejoiced in the punishment of a cruel villain.

Death of Godrich

Meanwhile Earl Godrich of Cornwall had heard with great uneasiness that Havelok had become King of Denmark and intended to invade England with a mighty army to assert his wife's right to the throne. He recognised that his own device to shame Goldborough had turned against him, and that he must now fight for his life and the usurped dominion he held over England. Godrich summoned his army to Lincoln for the defence of the realm against the Danes, and called out every man fit to bear weapons, on pain of becoming thrall if they failed him. Then he thus addressed them:

Friends, listen to my words, and you will know

'Tis not for sport, nor idle show, that I

Have bidden you to meet at Lincoln here.

Lo! here at Grimsby foreigners are come

Who have already won the Priory.

These Danes are cruel heathen, who destroy

Our churches and our abbeys: priests and nuns

They torture to the death, or lead away

To serve as slaves the haughty Danish jarls.

Now, Englishmen, what counsel will ye take?

If we submit, they will rule all our land,

Will kill us all, and sell our babes for thralls,

Will take our wives and daughters for their own.

Help me, if ever ye loved English land,

To fight these heathen and to cleanse our soil

From hateful presence of these alien hordes.

I make my vow to God and all the saints

I will not rest, nor houseled be, nor shriven,

Until our realm be free from Danish foe!

Accursed be he who strikes no blow for home!"

The army was inspired with valour by these courageous words, and the march to Grimsby began at once, with Earl Godrich in command. Havelok's men marched out gallantly to meet them, and when the battle joined many mighty deeds of valour were done, especially by the king himself, his foster-brothers, and Jarl Ubbe. The battle lasted long and was very fierce and bloody, but the Danes gradually overcame the resistance of the English, and at last, after a great hand-to-hand conflict, King Havelok captured Godrich. The traitor earl, who had lost a hand in the fray, was sent bound and fettered to Queen Goldborough, who kept him, carefully guarded, until he could be tried by his peers, since (for all his treason) he was still a knight.

When the English recognised their rightful lady and queen they did homage with great joy, begging mercy for having resisted their lawful ruler at the command of a wicked traitor; and the king and queen pardoned all but Godrich, who was speedily brought to trial at Lincoln. He was sentenced to be burnt at the stake, and the sentence was carried out amid general rejoicings.

Now that vengeance was satisfied, Havelok and his wife thought of recompensing the loyal helpers who had believed in them and supported them through the long years of adversity. Havelok married one of Grim's daughters to the Earl of Chester, and the other to Bertram, the good cook, who became Earl of Cornwall in the place of the felon Godrich and his disinherited children; the heroic Ubbe was made Regent of Denmark for Havelok, who decided to stay and rule England, and all the noble Danish warriors were rewarded with gifts of gold, and lands and castles. After a great coronation feast, which lasted for forty days, King Havelok dismissed the Danish regent and his followers, and after sad farewells they returned to their own country. Havelok and Goldborough ruled England in peace and security for sixty years, and lived together in all bliss, and had fifteen children, who all became mighty kings and queens.

HE WHO WOULD MARRY A FAIRY

Adapted from Welsh Folk-Lore by Owain Elias, published in 1896 by Woodall, Minshall and Co, and based on Elias' prize essay of the national Eisteddfod, 1887.

ONCE ON A TIME A SHEPHERD boy had gone up the mountain. That day, like many a day before and after, was exceedingly misty. Now, though he was well acquainted with the place, he lost his way, and walked backwards and forwards for many a long hour. At last he got into a low rushy spot, where he saw before him many circular rings. He at once recalled the place and began to fear the worst. He had heard, many hundreds of times, of the bitter experiences in those rings of many a shepherd who had happened to chance on the dancing-place or the circles of the Fair Family.

He hastened away as fast as ever he could, lest he should be ruined like the rest; but though he exerted himself to the point of perspiring, and losing his breath, there he was, and there he continued to be, a long time. At last he was met by a little fat old man with merry blue eyes, who asked him what he was doing. He answered that he was trying to find his way homeward.

"Oh," said he, "come after me, and do not utter a word until I bid thee." This the shepherd did, following the little fat old man on and on until they came to an oval stone, and the little fat old man lifted it, after tapping the middle of it three times with his walking stick. There was there a narrow path with stairs to be seen here and there, and a sort of whitish light, inclining to grey and blue, was to be seen radiating from the stones.

"Follow me fearlessly," said the fat man, "no harm will be done thee." So, on the poor youth went, as reluctantly as a dog to be hanged; but presently a fine-wooded, fertile country spread itself out before them, with well-arranged mansions dotting it over, while every kind of apparent magnificence met the eye, and seemed to smile in its landscape; the bright waters of its rivers meandered in twisted streams, and its hills were covered with the luxuriant verdure of their grassy growth, and the mountains with a glossy fleece of smooth pasture.

By the time they had reached the stout gentleman's mansion, the young man's senses had been bewildered by the sweet cadence of the music which the birds poured forth from the groves, then there was gold there to dazzle his eyes and silver flashing on his sight. He saw there all kinds of musical instruments and all sorts of things for playing, but he could discern no inhabitant in the whole place; and when he sat down to eat, the dishes on the table came to their places of themselves and disappeared when one had done with them.

This puzzled him beyond measure; moreover, he heard people talking together around him, but for the life of him he could see no one but his old friend. At length the fat man said to him, "You can now talk as much as it may please thee;" but when the shepherd attempted to move his tongue it would no more stir than if it had been a lump of ice, which greatly frightened him.

At this point, a fine old lady, with health and benevolence beaming in her face, came to them and slightly smiled at the shepherd. The mother was followed by her three daughters, who were remarkably beautiful. They gazed with somewhat playful looks at him, and at length began to talk to him, but his tongue would not wag. Then one of the girls came to him, and, playing with his yellow and curly locks, gave him a smart kiss on his ruddy lips. This loosened the string that bound his tongue, and he began to talk freely and eloquently.

There he was, under the charm of that kiss, in the bliss of happiness, and there he remained a year and a day without knowing that he had passed more than a day among them, for he had got into a country where there was no reckoning of time. But by and by he began to feel somewhat of a longing to visit his old home and asked the stout man if he might go.

"Stay a little yet," said he, "and you shall go for a while." That passed, he stayed on; but Olwen, for that was the name of the damsel that had kissed him, was very unwilling that he should depart. She looked sad every time he talked of going away, nor was he himself without feeling a sort of a cold thrill passing through him at the thought of leaving her. On condition, however, of returning, he obtained leave to go, provided with plenty of gold and silver, of trinkets and gems.

When he reached home, nobody knew who he was; it had been the belief that he had been killed by another shepherd, who found it necessary to betake himself hastily far away to America, lest he should be hanged without delay. But here was Einion Las at home, and everybody wondered specially to see that the shepherd had got to look like a wealthy man; his manners, his dress, his language, and the treasure he had with him, all conspired to give him the air of a gentleman.

The shepherd went back one Thursday night, the first of the moon that month, as suddenly as he had left the first time, and nobody knew whither. There was great joy in the country below when Einion returned thither, and nobody was more rejoiced at it than Olwen, his beloved. The two were right impatient to get married, but it was necessary to do that quietly, for the family below hated nothing more than fuss and noise; so, in a sort of a half-secret fashion, they were wedded.

Einion was very desirous to go once more among his own people, accompanied, to be sure, by his wife. After he had been long entreating the old man for leave, they set out on two white ponies, that were, in fact, more like snow than anything else in point of colour; so he arrived with his consort in his old home, and it was the opinion of all that Einion's wife was the handsomest person they had anywhere seen.

Whilst at home, a son was born to them, to whom they gave the name of Taliesin. Einion was now in the enjoyment of high repute, and his wife received proper respect. Their wealth was immense, and soon they acquired a large estate; but it was not long till people began to inquire after the pedigree of Einion's wife. The country was of the opinion that it was not the right thing to be without a pedigree. Einion was questioned about it, without his giving any satisfactory answer, and one came to the conclusion that she was one of the Fair Family (Tylwyth Têg).

"Certainly," replied Einion, "there can be no doubt that she comes from a very fair family, for she has two sisters who are as fair as she, and if you saw them together, you would admit that name to be a capital one."

This, then, is the reason why the remarkable family in the land of charm and phantasy (Hud a Lledrith) are called the Fair Family.

HOW THE CYMRY LAND BECAME INHABITED

Adapted from Welsh Fairy Tales by William Elliot Griffis and originally published in 1921.

In all Britain today, no wolf roams wild and the deer are all tame. Yet in the early ages, when human beings had not yet come into the land, the swamps and forests were full of very savage animals. There were bears and wolves by the thousand besides lions and the woolly rhinoceros, tigers, with terrible teeth like sabres.

Beavers built their dams over the little rivers, and the great horned oxen were very common. Then the mountains were higher, and the woods denser. Many of the animals lived in caves, and there were billions of bees and a great many butterflies. In the bogs were ferns of giant size, amid which terrible monsters hid that were always ready for a fight or a frolic. In so beautiful a land, it seemed a pity that there were no men and women, no boys or girls, and no babies.

Yet the noble race of the Cymry, whom we call the Welsh, were already in Europe and lived in the summer land in the South. A great benefactor was born among them, who grew up to be a wonderfully wise man and taught his people the use of bows and arrows. He made laws, by which the different tribes stopped their continual fighting and quarrels, and united for the common good of all. He persuaded them to take family names. He invented the plough, and showed them how to use it, making furrows, in which to plant grain.

When the people found that they could get things to eat right out of the ground, from the seed they had planted, their children were wild with joy. No people ever loved babies more than these Cymry folk and it was they who invented the cradle. This saved the hard-working mothers many a burden, for each woman had, besides rearing the children, to work for and wait on her husband.

He was the warrior and hunter, and she did most of the labour, in both the house and the field. When there were many little brats to look after, a cradle was a real help to her. In those days, "brat" was the general name for little folks. There were good laws, about women especially for their protection. Any rough or brutish fellow was fined heavily, or publicly punished, for striking one of them.

By and by, this great benefactor encouraged his people to the brave adventure, and led them, in crossing the sea to Britain. Men had not yet learned to build boats, with prow or stern, with keels and masts, or with sails, rudders, or oars, or much less to put engines in their bowels, or iron chimneys for smoke stacks, by which we see the mighty ships driven across the ocean without regard to wind or tide.

This great benefactor taught his people to make coracles, and on these the whole tribe of thousands of Cymric folk crossed over into Britain, landing in Cornwall. The old name of this shire meant the Horn of Gallia, or Wallia, as the new land was later named. We think of Cornwall as the big toe of the Motherland. These first comers called it a horn. It was a funny sight to see these coracles, which they named after their own round bodies. The men went down to the riverside or the sea shore, and with their stone hatchets, they chopped down trees. They cut the reeds and osiers, peeled the willow branches, and wove great baskets shaped like bowls. In this work, the women helped the men.

The coracle was made strong by a wooden frame fixed inside round the edge, and by two cross boards, which also served as seats. Then they turned the wicker frame upside down and stretched the hides of animals over the whole frame and bottom. With pitch, gum, or grease, they covered up the cracks or seams. Then they shaped paddles out of wood. When the coracle floated on the water, the whole family, daddy, mammy, kiddies, and any old aunts or uncles, or granddaddies, got into it. They waited for the wind to blow from the south over to the northern land. At first the coracle spun round and round, but by and by each daddy could, by rowing or paddling, make the thing go straight ahead. So, finally all arrived in the land now called Great Britain.

Though sugar was not then known, or for a thousand years later, the first thing they noticed was the enormous number of bees. When they searched, they found the rock caves and hollow trees full of honey, which had accumulated for generations. Every once in a while, the bears, that so like sweet things, found out the hiding place of the bees, and ate up the honey. The children were very happy in sucking the honey comb and the mothers made candles out of the beeswax. The newcomers named the country Honey Island.

The brave Cymry men had battles with the darker skinned people who were already there. When any one, young or old, died, their friends and relatives sat up all night guarding the body against wild beasts or savage men. This grew to be a settled custom and such a meeting was called a "wake'. Everyone present did keep awake, and often in a very lively way.

As the Cymry multiplied, they built many don, or towns. All over the land today are names ending in don like London, or Croydon, showing where these villages were. But while occupied in things for the body, their great ruler did not neglect matters of the mind. He found that some of his people had good voices and loved to sing. Others delighted in making poetry. So, he invented or improved the harp, and fixed the rules of verse and song. Thus, ages before writing was known, the Cymry preserved their history and handed down what the wise ones taught.

Men might be born, live and die, come and go, like leaves on the trees, which expand in the springtime and fall in the autumn; but their songs, and poetry, and noble language never die. Even today, the Cymry love the speech of their fathers almost as well as they love their native land.

Yet things were not always lovely in Honey Land, or as sweet as sugar. As the tribes scattered far apart to settle in this or that valley, some had fish, but no salt, and others had plenty of salt, but no fish. Some had all the venison and bear meat they wanted, but no barley or oats. The hill men needed what the men on the seashore could supply. From their sheep and oxen, they got wool and leather, and from the wild beasts they took fur to keep warm in winter. So many of them grew expert in trade. Soon there were among them some very rich men who were the chiefs of the tribes.

In time, hundreds of others learned how to traffic among the tribes and swap, or barter their goods, for as yet there were no coins for money, or bank bills. So, they established markets or fairs, to which the girls and boys liked to go and sell their eggs and chickens, for when the wolves and foxes were killed off, sheep and geese multiplied.

But what hindered the peace of the land, were the feuds, or quarrels, because the men of one tribe thought they were braver, or better looking, than those in the other tribe. The women were very apt to boast that they wore their clothes, which were made of fox and weasel skins, more gracefully than those in the tribe next to them.

So, there was much snarling and quarrelling in Cymric Land. The people were too much like naughty children, or when kiddies are not taught good manners, to speak gently and to be kind one to the other. One of the worst quarrels broke out, because in one tribe there were too many maidens and not enough young men for husbands. This was bad for the men, for it spoiled them. They had too many women to wait on them and they grew to be very selfish.

In what might be the next tribe, the trouble was the other way. There were too many boys, a surplus of men, and not nearly enough girls to go around. When any young fellow, moping out his life alone and anxious for a wife, went a-courting in the next tribe, or in their vale, or on their hilltop, he was usually driven off with stones. Then there was a quarrel between the two tribes.

Any young girl, who sneaked out at night to meet her young man of another clan, was, when caught, instantly and severely chastised. Then, humiliated, she had to stand tied to a post in the marketplace a whole day. Her hair was pulled down in disorder, and all the dogs were allowed to bark at her. The girls made fun of the poor thing, while they all rubbed one forefinger over the other, pointed at her and cried, "Fie, for shame!" while the boys called her hard names.

If it were known that the young man who wanted a wife had visited a girl in the other tribe, his spear and bow and arrows were taken away from him till the moon was full. The other boys and the girls treated him roughly and called him hard names, but he dare not defend himself and had to suffer patiently. This was all because of the feud between the two tribes.

This went on until the maidens in the valley, who were very many, while yet lovely and attractive, became very lonely and miserable; while the young men, all splendid hunters and warriors, multiplied in the hill country. They were wretched in mind, because not one could get a wife, for all the maidens in their own tribe were already engaged or had been wed.

One day news came to the young men on the hill top, that the valley men were all off on a hunting expedition. At once, without waiting a moment, the poor lonely bachelors plucked up courage. Then, armed with ropes and straps, they marched in a body to the village in the valley below. There, they seized each man a girl, not waiting for any maid to comb her hair, or put on a new frock, or pack up her clothes, or carry anything out of her home, and made off with her, as fast as one pair of legs could move with another pair on top.

At first, this looked like rough treatment, for a lovely girl, thus to be strapped to a brawny big fellow; but after a while, the girls thought it was great fun to be married and each one to have a man to caress, and fondle, and scold, and look for, and boss around; for each wife, inside of her own hut was quite able to rule her husband. Every one of these new wives was delighted to find a man who cared so much for her as to come after her, and risk his life to get her, and each one admired her new, brave husband.

Yet the brides knew too well that their men folks, fathers and brothers, uncles and cousins, would soon come back to attempt their recapture. And this was just what happened. When a runner brought, to the valley men now far away, the news of the taking of their daughters, the hunters at once ceased chasing the deer and marched quickly back to get the girls and make them come home.

The hill men saw the band of hunters coming after their daughters. They at once took their new wives into a natural rocky fortress, on the top of a precipice, which overlooked the lake.

This stronghold had only one entrance, a sort of gateway of rocks, in front of which was a long steep, narrow path. Here the hill men stood, to resist the attack and hold their prizes. It was a case of a very few defenders, assaulted by a multitude, and the battle was long and bloody. The hill men scorned to surrender and shot their arrows and hurled their javelins with desperate valour. They battled all day from sunrise until the late afternoon, when shadows began to lengthen. The stars, one by one came out and both parties, after setting sentinels, lay down to rest.

In the morning, again, charge after charge was made. Sword beat against shield and helmet, and clouds of arrows were shot by the archers, who were well posted in favourable situations, on the rocks. Long before noon, the field below was dotted and the narrow pass was choked with dead bodies. In the afternoon, after a short rest and refreshed with food, the valley men, though finding that only four of the hill fighters were alive, stood off at a distance and with their long bows and a shower of arrows left not one to breathe.

Now, thought the victors, we shall get our maidens back again. So, taking their time to wash off the blood and dust, to bind up their wounds, and to eat their supper, they thought it would be an easy job to load up all the girls on their ox-carts and carry them home. But the valley brides, thus suddenly made widows, were too true to their brave husbands. So, when they had seen the last of their lovers quiet in death, they stripped off all their ornaments and fur robes, until all stood together, each clad in her own innocence, as pure in their purpose as if they were a company of Druid priestesses.

Then, chanting their death song, they marched in procession to the tall cliff, that rose sheer out of the water. One by one, each uttering the name of her beloved, leaped into the waves.

Men at a distance, knowing nothing of the fight, and sailors and fishermen far off on the water, thought that a flock of white birds were swooping down from their eyrie, into the sea to get their food from the fishes. But when none rose up above the waters, they understood, and later heard the whole story of the valour of the men and the devotion of the women.

The solemn silence of night soon brooded over the scene. The men of the valley stayed only long enough to bury their own dead. Then they marched home and their houses were filled with mourning. Yet they admired the noble sacrifice of their daughters and were proud of them. Afterwards they raised stone monuments on the field of slaughter. Today, this water is called the Lake of the Maidens, and the great stones seen near the beach are the memorials marking the place of the slain in battle.

During many centuries, the ancient custom of capturing the bride, with resistance from her male relatives, was vigorously kept up. In the course of time, however, this was turned into a mimic play, with much fun and merriment.

KADDY'S LUCK

*Adapted from Fairy-Tales & Other Stories by Peter Henry Emerson,
published by D. Nutt, London in 1894.*

THERE WAS A TALL YOUNG WOMAN whom the fairies used to visit, coming through the keyhole at night. She could hear them dancing and singing in her room, but in the morning, they used to go the way they had come, only they always left her some money.

When she got married she chose a tall husband like herself, and they had a fine big child.

One night they went to a fair, and they got to one side to hear the fairies; for some people could tell when the fairies were coming, for they made a noise like the wind. Whilst they were waiting she told her husband how the fairies used to leave her money at night.

When they got home they found their baby all right and went to bed. But next morning the young mother found her child had been changed in the night, and there was a very little baby in the cradle. And the child never grew big, for the fairies had changed her child for spite.

Tales From The Land Of Dragons

KING ARTHUR'S CAVE

Adapted from Welsh Fairy Tales by William Elliot Griffis and originally published in 1921.

IN OLD DAYS PEOPLE MADE USE of the forked branches of the hazel as a divining rod. With this, they believed that they could divine, or find out the presence of treasures of gold and silver, deep down in the earth, and hidden from human eyes. Our story is about a hazel rod, a Welshman on London Bridge, treasures in a cave, and what happened because of these.

It was in the days when London Bridge was not, as we see it today, a massive structure of stone and iron, able to bear up hundreds of cars, wagons, horses and people, and lighted at night with electric bulbs. No, when this particular Welshman visited London, the bridge had a line of shops on both sides of the passageway, reaching from one end right to the other end.

Taffy was the name of this fellow from Denbigh, in Wales, and he was a drover. He had brought, all the way from one of the richest of the Welsh provinces, a great drove of Black Welsh cattle, such as were in steady demand by Englishmen, who have always been lovers of roast beef. Escaping all the risks of cattle thieves, rustlers, and highwaymen, he had sold his beeves at a good price; so that his pockets were now fairly bulging out with gold coins, and yet this fellow wanted more. But first, before going home, he would see the sights of the great city, which then contained about a hundred thousand people.

While he was handling some things in a shop, to decide what he should take home to his wife, his three daughters and his two little boys, he noticed a man looking intently, not at him, but at his stick. After a while, the stranger came up to him and asked him where he came from.

Now Taffy was not very refined in his manners, and he thought it none of the fellow's business. He was very surly and made reply in a gruff voice. "I come from my own country."

The stranger did not get angry, but in a polite tone made answer. "Don't be offended at my question. Tell me where you cut that hazel stick, and I'll make it to your advantage, if you will take my advice."

Even yet Taffy was gruff and suspicious. "What business is it of yours, where I cut my hazel stick?" he answered.

"Well it may matter a good deal to you, if you will tell me. For, if you remember the place, and can lead me to it, I'll make you a rich man, for near that spot lies a great treasure."

Taffy was not much of a thinker, apart from matters concerning cattle, and his brain worked slowly! He was sorely puzzled. Here was a wizard, who could make him rich, and he did so love to jingle gold in his pockets. But then he was superstitious. He feared that this sorcerer derived all his uncanny knowledge from demons, and Taffy, being rather much of a sinner, feared these very much. Meanwhile, his new acquaintance kept on persuading him. Finally, Taffy yielded and the two went on together to Wales.

Now in this country, there are many stones placed in position, showing they were not there by accident, but were reared by men, to mark some old battle, or famous event. And for this, rough stone work, no country, unless it be Korea or China, is more famous than Wales. On reaching one called the Fortress Rock, Taffy pointed to an old hazel root, and said to his companion, "There! From that stock, I cut my hazel stick. I am sure of it."

The sorcerer looked at Taffy to read his face, and to be certain that he was telling the truth. Then he said, "Bring shovels and we'll both dig."

These having been brought, the two began to work until the perspiration stood out in drops on their foreheads. First the sod and rooty stuff, and then down around the gravelly mass below, they plied their digging tools. Taffy was not used to such toil, and his muscles were soon weary. But, urged on by visions of gold, he kept bravely at his task. At last, when ready to drop from fatigue, he heard his companion say, "We've struck it!"

A few shovelfuls more laid bare a broad flat stone. This they pried up, but it required all their strength to lift and stand it on edge. Just below, they saw a flight of steps. They were slippery with wet and they looked very old, as if worn, ages ago, by many feet passing up and down them. Taffy shrunk back, as a draught of the close, dead air struck his nostrils.

"Come on, and don't be afraid. I'm going to make you rich," said the sorcerer.

At this, Taffy's eyes glistened, and he followed on down the steps, without saying a word. At the bottom of the descent, they entered a narrow passage, and finally came to a door.

"Now, I'll ask you. Are you brave, and will you come in with me, if I open this door?"

By this time, Taffy was so eager for treasure, that he spoke up at once. "I'm not afraid. Open the door."

The sorcerer gave a jerk and the door flew open. What a sight! There, in the faint, red light, Taffy discerned a great cave. Lying on the floor were hundreds of armed men, but motionless and apparently sound asleep. Little spangles of light were reflected from swords, spears, round shields, and burnished helmets. All these seemed of very ancient pattern. But immediately in front of them was a bell. Taffy felt some curiosity to tap it. Would the sleeping host of men then rise up?

Just then, the sorcerer, speaking with a menacing gesture, and in a harsh tone, said, "Do not touch that bell, or it's all up with us both."

Moving carefully, so as not to trip, or to stumble over the sleeping soldiers, they went on, and Taffy, stopping and looking up beheld before him a great round table. Many warriors were sitting at it. Their splendid gold inlaid armour, glittering helmets and noble faces showed that they were no common men. Yet Taffy could see only a few of the faces, for all had their heads more or less bent down, as if sound asleep, though sword and spear were near at hand, ready to be grasped in a moment.

Outshining all, was a golden throne at the farther end of the table and on it sat a king. He was of imposing stature, and august presence. Upon his head was a crown, on which were inlaid or set precious stones. These shone by their own light, sending out rays so brilliant that they dazzled Taffy, who had never seen anything like them. The king held in his right hand a mighty sword. It had a history and the name of it was Excalibur. In Arthur's hand, it was almost part of his own soul. Its hilt and handle were of finely chased gold, richly studded with gems. Yet his head, too, was bent in deep sleep, as if only thunder could wake him.

"Are they all, everyone, asleep?" asked Taffy.

"Each and all," was the answer.

"When did they fall asleep?" asked the drover.

"Over a thousand years ago," answered the sorcerer.

"Tell me who they are, and why here," asked Taffy.

"They are King Arthur's trusty warriors. They are waiting for the hour to come, when they shall rise up and destroy the enemies of the Cymry, and once again possess the whole island of Britain, as in the early ages, before the Saxons came."

"And who are those sitting around the table?" asked Taffy.

The sorcerer seemed tired of answering questions, but he replied, giving the name of each knight, and also that of his father, as if he were a Welshman himself; but at this, Taffy grew impatient, feeling as if a book of genealogy had been hurled at him.

Most impolitely, he interrupted his companion and cried out, "And who is that on the throne?"

The sorcerer looked as if he was vexed, and felt insulted, but he answered, "It's King Arthur himself, with Excalibur, his famous sword, in his hand." This was snapped out, as if the sorcerer was disgusted at the interruption of his genealogy, and he shut his mouth tight as if he would answer no more questions, for such an impolite fellow.

Seizing Taffy by the hand, he led him into what was the storehouse of the cave. There lay heaps upon heaps of yellow gold. Both men stuffed their pockets, belt bags, and the inside of their clothes, with all they could load in.

"Now we had better get out, for it is time to go," said the sorcerer and he led the way towards the cave door.

But as Taffy passed back, and along the hall, where the host of warriors were sleeping, his curiosity got the better of him. He said to himself, "I must see this host awake. I'll touch that bell and find out whether the sorcerer spoke the truth."

So, when he came to it, he struck the bell. In the twinkling of an eye, thousands of warriors sprang up, seized their armour, girded their swords, or seized their spears. All seemed eagerly awaiting the command to rush against the foe.

The ground quaked with their tramping, and shook with their tread, until Taffy thought the cave roof would fall in and bury them all. The air resounded with the rattle of arms, as the men, when in ranks, marked time, ready for motion forward and out of the cave.

But from the midst of the host, a deep sounding voice, as earnest as if in hot temper, but as deliberate as if in caution against a false alarm, spoke. He inquired, "Who rang that bell? Has the day come?"

The sorcerer, thoroughly frightened and trembling, answered, "No, the day has not come. Sleep on."

Taffy, though dazzled by the increasing brilliancy of the light, had heard another deep voice, more commanding in its tones than even a king's, call out, "Arthur, awake, the bell has rung. The day is breaking. Awake, great King Arthur!"

But even against such a voice, that of the sorcerer, now scared beyond measure, lest the king and his host should discover the cheat, and with his sword, Excalibur, chop the heads off both Taffy and himself, answered, "No, it is still night. Sleep on, Arthur the Great."

Erect over all, his head aloft and crowned with jewels, as with stars, the King himself now spoke, "No, my warriors, the day has not yet come, when the Black Eagle and the Golden Eagle will meet in war. Sleep on, loyal souls. The morning of Wales has not yet dawned."

Then, like the gentle soughing of the evening breeze among forest trees, all sound died away, and in the snap of a finger, all were asleep again. Seizing the hand of Taffy, the sorcerer hurried him out of the cave, moved the stone back in its place and motioning to Taffy to do the same, he quickly shovelled and kicked the loose dirt in the hole and stamped it down: When Taffy turned to look for him, he was gone, without even taking the trouble to call his dupe a fool.

Wearied with his unwonted labours and excitements, Taffy walked home, got his supper, pondered on what he had seen, slept, and awoke in the morning refreshed. After breakfast, he sallied out again with pick and shovel.

For months, Taffy dug over every square foot of the hill. Neglecting his business as cattle man, he spent all the money he had made in London, but he never found that entrance to the cave. He died a poor man and all his children had to work hard to get their bread.

OLD GWILYM

Adapted from Fairy-Tales & Other Stories by Peter Henry Emerson,
published by D. Nutt, London in 1894.

OLD GWILYM EVANS STARTED OFF ONE fine morning to walk across the Eagle Hills to a distant town, bent upon buying some cheese. On his way, in a lonely part of the hills, he found a golden guinea, which he quickly put into his pocket.

When he got to the town, instead of buying his provisions, he went into an alehouse, and sat drinking and singing with some sweet-voiced quarrymen until dark, when he thought it was time to go home. Whilst he was drinking, an old woman with a basket came in, and sat beside him, but she left before him.

After the parting glass he got up and reeled through the town, quite forgetting to buy his cheese; and as he got amongst the hills they seemed to dance up and down before him, and he seemed to be walking on air. When he got near the lonely spot where he had found the money he heard some sweet music, and a number of fairies crossed his path and began dancing all round him, and then as he looked up he saw some brightly-lighted houses before him on the hill; and he scratched his head, for he never remembered having seen houses thereabouts before. And as he was thinking, and watching the fairies, one came and begged him to come into the house and sit down.

So, he followed her in, and found the house was all gold inside it, and brightly lighted, and the fairies were dancing and singing, and they brought him anything he wanted for supper, and then they put him to bed.

Gwilym slept heavily, and when he awoke turned around, for he felt very cold, and his body seemed covered with prickles; so, he sat up and rubbed his eyes, and found that he was quite naked and lying in a bunch of gorse.

When he found himself in this plight he hurried home, and told his wife, and she was very angry with him for spending all the money and bringing no cheese home, and then he told her his adventures.

"Oh, you bad man!" she said, "the fairies gave you money and you spent it wrongly, so they were sure to take their revenge."

ORIGIN OF THE WELSH

Adapted from Fairy-Tales & Other Stories by Peter Henry Emerson,
published by D. Nutt, London in 1894.

MANY YEARS AGO, THERE LIVED SEVERAL wild tribes round the King of Persia's city, and the king's men were always annoying and harassing them, exacting yearly a heavy tribute. Now these tribes, though very brave in warfare, could not hold their own before the Persian army when sent out against them, so that they paid their yearly tribute grudgingly, but took revenge, whenever they could, upon travellers to or from the city, robbing and killing them.

At last one of the tribesmen, a clever old chieftain, thought of a cunning plan whereby to defeat the Persians, and free themselves from the yearly tribute. And this was his scheme:

The wild wastes where these tribes lived were infested with large birds called "Rohs", which were very destructive to human beings, devouring men, women, and children greedily whenever they could catch them. Such a terror were they that the tribes had to protect their village with high walls, and then they slept securely, for the Roh hunted by night. This old chieftain determined to watch the birds and find out their nesting-places; so he had a series of towers built, in which the watchmen could sleep securely by night. These towers were advanced in whatever direction the birds were seen to congregate by night. The observers reported that the Roh could not fly, but ran very swiftly, being fleeter than any horse.

At length, by watching, their nesting-places were found in a sandy plain, and it was discovered that those monstrous birds stole sheep and cattle in great numbers. The chieftain then gave orders for the watchmen to keep on guard until the young birds were hatched, when they were commanded to secure fifty, and bring them into the walled town. The order was carried out, and one night they secured fifty young birds just out of the egg and brought them to the town.

The old chieftain then chose fifty skilful warriors, a man to each bird, to his son being allotted the largest bird. These warriors were ordered to feed the birds on flesh, and to train them for battle. The birds grew up as tame as horses. Saddles and bridles were made for them, and they were trained and exercised just like chargers.

When the next tribute day came around, the King of Persia sent his emissaries to collect the tax, but the chieftains of the tribes insulted and defied them, so that they returned to the king, who at once sent forward his army.

The chieftain then marshalled his men, and forty-six of the Rohs were drawn up in front of the army, the chief getting on the strongest bird. The remaining four were placed on the right flank and ordered at a signal to advance and cut off the army, should they retreat.

The Rohs had small scales, like those of a fish, on their necks and bodies, the scales being hidden under a soft hair, except on the upper half of the neck. They had no feathers except on their wings. So, they were invulnerable except as to the eyes - for in those days the Persians only had bows and arrows, and light javelins. When the Persian army advanced, the Rohs advanced at lightning speed, and made fearful havoc, the birds murdering and trampling the soldiers under foot, and beating them down with their powerful wings. In less than two hours half the Persian army was slain, and the rest had escaped. The tribes returned to their walled towns, delighted with their victory.

When the news of his defeat reached the King of Persia he was wroth beyond expression and could not sleep for rage. So, the next morning he called for his magician.

"What are you going to do with the birds?" asked the king.

"Well, I've been thinking the matter over," replied the magician.

"Cannot you destroy all of them?"

"No, your majesty; I cannot destroy them, for I have not the power; but I can get rid of them in one way; for though I cannot put out life, I have the power of turning one life into some other living creature."

"Well, what will you turn them into?" asked the king.

"I'll consider to-night, your majesty," replied the magician.

"Well, mind and be sure to do it."

"Yes, I'll be sure to do it, your majesty."

The next day, at ten, the magician appeared before the king, who asked, "Have you considered well?"

"Yes, your majesty."

"Well, how are you going to act?"

"Your majesty, I've thought and thought during the night, and the best thing we can do is to turn all the birds into fairies."

"What are fairies?" asked the king.

"I've planned it all out, and I hope your majesty will agree."

"Oh! I'll agree, as long as they never molest us more."

"Well, your majesty, I'm going to turn them to fairies - small living creatures to live in caves in the bowels of the earth, and they shall only visit people living on the earth once a year. They shall be harmless, and hurt nothing; they shall be fairies, and do nothing but dance and sing, and I shall allow them to go about on earth for twenty-four hours once a year and play their antics, but they shall do no mischief."

"How long are the birds to remain in that state?" asked the king.

"I'll give them two thousand years, your majesty; and at the end of that time they are to go back into birds, as they were before. And after the birds change from the fairy state back into birds, they shall never breed more, but die a natural death."

So the tribes lost their birds, and the King of Persia made such fearful havoc amongst them that they decided to leave the country.

They travelled, supporting themselves by robbery; until they came to a place where they built a city, and called it Troy, where they were besieged for a long time.

At length the besiegers built a large caravan, with a large man's head in front; the head was all gilded with gold. When the caravan was finished they put 150 of the best warriors inside, provided with food, and one of them had a trumpet. Then they pulled the caravan, which ran upon eight broad wheels, up to the gates of the city, and left it there, their army being drawn up in a valley nearby. It was, agreed that when the caravan got inside the gates the bugler should blow three loud blasts to warn, the army, who would immediately advance into the city.

The men on the ramparts saw this curious caravan, and they began wondering what it was, and for two or three days they left it alone.

At last an old chieftain said, "It must be their food."

On the third day they opened the gates, and attaching ropes, began to haul it into the city; then the warriors leaped out, and the horn blew, and the army hurried up, and the town was taken after great slaughter; but a number escaped with their wives and children, and fled on to the Crimea, whence they were driven by the Russians, so they marched away along the sea to Spain, and bearing up through France, they stopped. Some wanted to go across the sea, and some stayed in the heart of France: they were the Bretons. The others came on over in boats, and landed in England, and they were the first people settled in Great Britain: they were the Welsh.

POWELL, PRINCE OF DYFED

Adapted from Welsh Fairy Tales by William Elliot Griffis and originally published in 1921.

ONE OF THE OLDEST OF THE Welsh fairy tales tells us about Pwyle, King of Fairyland and father of the numerous clan of the Powells. He was a mighty hunter. He could ride a horse, draw a bow, and speak the truth. He was always honoured by men, and he kept his faith and his promises to women. The children loved him, for he loved them. In the castle hall, he could tell the best stories. No man, bard, or warrior, foot holder or commoner, could excel him in gaining and keeping the attention of his hearers, even when they were sleepy and wanted to go to bed.

One day, when out a hunting in the woods, Powell noticed a pack of hounds running down a stag. He saw at once that they were not his own, for they were snow white in colour and had red ears. Being a young man, Powell did not know at this time of his life, that red is the fairy colour, and that these were all dogs from Fairyland. So, he drove off the red-eared hounds, and was about to let loose his own pack on the stag, when a horseman appeared on the scene.

The stranger at once began to upbraid Powell for being impolite. He asked why his hounds should not be allowed to hunt the deer.

Powell spoke pleasantly in reply, making his proper excuses to the horseman. The two began to like each other, and soon got acquainted and mutually enjoyed being companions.

It turned out that the stranger was Arawn, a king in Fairyland. He had a rival named Hargan, who was beating him and his army in war. So Arawn asked Powell to help him against his enemy. He even made request that one year from that time, Powell should meet Hargan in battle. He told him that one stroke of his sword would finish the enemy. He must then sheathe his weapon, and not, on any account, strike a second time.

To make victory sure, the Fairy King would exchange shapes with the mortal ruler and each take not only the place, but each the shape and form of the other. Powell must go into Fairy Land and govern the kingdom there, while Arawn should take charge of affairs at Dyfed.

But Powell was warned, again, to smite down his enemy with a single stroke of his sword. If, in the heat of the conflict, and the joy of victory, Powell should forget, and give a second blow to Hargan, he would immediately come to life and be as strong as ever.

Powell heeded well these words. Then, putting on the shape of Arawn, he went into Fairy Land, and no one noticed, or thought of anything different from the days and years gone by. But now, at night, a new and unexpected difficulty arose. Arawn's beautiful wife was evidently not in the secret, for she greeted Powell as her own husband.

After dinner, when the telling of stories in the banqueting hall was over, the time had come for them to retire. But the new bed fellow did not even kiss her, or say "good night," but turned his back to her and his face to the wall, and never moved until daylight. Then the new King in Fairy Land rose up, ate his breakfast, and went out to hunt.

Every day, he ruled the castle and kingdom, as if he had always been the monarch. To everybody, he seemed as if he had been long used to public business, and no questions were asked, nor was there any talk made on the subject. Everyone took things as matter of course. Yet, however polite or gracious he might be to the queen during the day, in the evening, he spoke not a word, and passed every night as at the first.

The twelve months soon sped along, and now the time for the battle in single combat between Powell and Hargan had fully come. The two warriors met in the middle of a river ford and backed their horses for a charge. Then they rushed furiously at the other. Powell's spear struck Hargan so hard, that he was knocked out of the saddle and hurled, the length of a lance, over and beyond the crupper, or tail strap of his horse. He fell mortally wounded upon the ground.

Now came the moment of danger and temptation to Powell, for Hargan cried out, "For the love of Heaven, finish your work on me. Slay me with your sword."

But Powell was wise, and his head was cool. He had kept in mind the warning to strike only one blow. He called out loudly, so that all could hear him, "I will not repeat that. Slay you who may, I shall not."

So Hargan, knowing his end had come, bade his nobles bear him away from the river shore.

Then Powell, with his armies, overran the two kingdoms of Fairy Land and made himself master of all. He took oath of all the princes and nobles, who swore to be loyal to their new master. This done, Powell rode away to the trysting place in a glen, and there he met Arawn, as had been appointed. They changed shapes, and each became himself, as he had been before.

Arawn thanked Powell heartily, and bade him see what he had done for him. Then each one rode back, in his former likeness, to his kingdom.

Now at Anwyn, no one but Arawn himself knew that anything unusual had taken place. After dinner, and the evening storytelling were over, and it was time to go to bed, Arawn's wife was surprised in double measure.

Two things puzzled her. Her husband was now very tender to her and also very talkative; whereas, for a whole year, every night, he had been as silent and immovable as a log. How could it be, in either case?

But this time, the wife was silent as a statue. Even though Arawn spoke to her three times, he received no reply. Then he asked directly of her, why she was so silent. She made an answer that, for a whole year, no word had been spoken in their bedroom.

"What?" said he, "did we not talk together, as always before?"

"No," said she, "not for a year has there been talk or caress between us."

At this answer, Arawn was overcome with surprise, and as struck with admiration at having so good a friend. He burst out first in praise of Powell, and then told his wife all that had happened during the past twelve months. She, too, was full of admiration, and told her husband that in Powell he had certainly found a true friend.

In Dyfed, when Powell had returned to his own land and castle, he called his lords together. Then he asked them to be perfectly frank and free to speak. They must tell him whether they thought him a good king during the year past.

All shouted in chorus of approval. Then their spokesman addressed Powell thus: "My lord, never was your wisdom so great, your generosity more free, nor your justice more manifest, than during the past year." When he ceased, all the vassals showed their approval of this speech.

Then Powell, smiling, told the story of his adventures in exchanging his form and tasks; at the end of which, the spokesman taking his cue from the happy faces of all his fellow vassals, made reply, "Of a truth, lord, we pray thee, do you give thanks to Heaven that you have formed such a fellowship. Please continue to us the form of the kingdom and rule, that we have enjoyed for a year past."

Thereupon King Powell took oath, kissing the hilt of his sword, and called on Heaven to witness his promise that he would do as they had desired. So, the two kings confirmed the friendship they had made. Each sent the other rich gifts of jewels, horses and hounds.

In memory of so wonderful and happy union, of a mortal and a fairy, Powell was thereafter, in addition to all his titles, saluted as Lord of Anwyn, which is only another name for the Land of the Fairies.

POWELL AND HIS BRIDE

Adapted from Welsh Fairy Tales by William Elliot Griffis and originally published in 1921.

NOT FAR FROM THE CASTLE WHERE King Powell had his court, there was a hillock called the Mount of Macbeth. It was the common belief that some strange adventure would befall anyone who should sit upon that mound. He would receive blows, or wounds, or else he would see something wonderful.

Thus, it came to pass, that none but peaceful bards had ever sat upon the mound. Never a warrior or a common man had risked sitting there. The general fear felt, and the awe inspired by the place, was too great.

But after his adventure of being King of Fairy Land for a whole year, everything else to Powell seemed dull and commonplace. So, to test his own courage, and worthiness of kingship, Powell assembled all his lords at Narberth. After the night's feasting, revelry and storytelling, Powell declared that, next day, he would sit upon the enchanted mound.

So, when the sun was fully risen, Powell took his seat upon the mound, expecting that, all of a sudden, something unusual would happen. For some minutes nothing, whether event or vision, took place. Then he lifted up his eyes and saw approaching him a white horse on which rode a lady. She was dressed in shining garments, as if made of gold. Evidently, she was a princess. Yet she came not very near.

"Does anyone among you know who this lady is?" asked Powell of his chieftains.

"Not one of us," was the answer.

Thereupon Powell ordered his vassals to ride forward. They were to greet her courteously and inquire who she was. But now the predicted wonder took place. She moved away from them, yet at a quiet pace that suited her. Though the knights spurred their horses, and rode fast and furiously, they could not come any nearer to her. They galloped back and reported their failure to reach the lady.

Then Powell picked out others and sent them riding after the lady, but each time, one and all returned, chagrined with failure. A woman had beaten them. So the day closed with silence in the castle hall. There was no merry making or story telling that night.

The next day, Powell sat again on the mound and once more the golden lady came near. This time, Powell himself left his seat on the mound, leaped on his fleetest horse, and pursued the maiden, robed in gold, on the white horse. But she flitted away, as she had done before from the knights. Again and again, though he could get nearer and nearer to her, he failed.

Then the baffled king cried out, in despair, "O maiden fair, for the sake of him whom you lovest, stay for me."

Evidently the lady, who lived in the time of castles and courts, did not care to be wooed in the style of the cave men. Such manners did not suit her, but with a change of method of making love, her heart melted. Besides, she was a kind woman. She took pity on horses, as well as on men.

Sweet was her voice, as she answered most graciously, "I will stay gladly, and it were better for your horses, had you asked me properly, long ago."

To his questions, as to how and why she came to him, she told her story, as follows: "I am Rhiannon, descended from the August and Venerable One of old. My aunts and uncles tried to make me marry against my will a chieftain named Gwawl, an auburn-haired youth, son of Clud, but, because of my love to thee, would I have no husband, and if you reject me, I will never marry any man."

"As Heaven is my witness, were I to choose among all the damsels and ladies of the world, you would I choose," cried Powell.

After that, it was agreed that, when a year had sped, Powell should go to the Palace of the August and Venerable One of old and claim her for his bride. So, when twelve months had passed, Powell with his retinue of a hundred knights, all splendidly horsed and finely apparelled, presented himself before the castle. There he found his fair lady and a feast already prepared at which he sat with her. On the other side of the table, were her father and mother.

In the midst of this joyous occasion, when all was gayety, and they talked together, in strode a youth clad in sheeny satin. He was of noble bearing and had auburn hair. He saluted Powell and his knights courteously.

At once Powell, the lord of Narberth, invited the stranger to come and sit down as guest beside him.

"Not so," replied the youth. "I am a suitor and have come to crave a boon of thee."

Without guile or suspicion, Powell replied innocently, "Ask what you will. If in my power, it shall be yours."

But Rhiannon chided Powell. She asked, "Oh, why did you give him such an answer?"

"But he did give it," cried the auburn-haired youth. Then turning to the whole company of nobles, he appealed to them, "Did he not pledge his word, before you all, to give me what I asked?"

Then, turning to Powell, he said, "The boon I ask is this, to have your bride, Rhiannon. Further, I want this feast and banquet to celebrate, in this place, our wedding."

At this demand, Powell seemed to have been struck dumb. He did not speak, but Rhiannon did. "Be silent, as long as you wilt," she cried, "but surely no man ever made worse use of his wits than you have done; for this man, to whom you gave your oath of promise, is none other than Gwawl, the son of Clud. He is the suitor, from whom I fled to come to you, while you sat on the Narberth mound."

Now, out of such trouble, how should the maiden, promised to two men, be delivered?

Her wit saved her for the nonce. Powell was bound to keep his word; but Rhiannon explained to Gwawl, that it was not his castle or hall. So, he could not give the banquet; but, in a year from that date, if Gwawl would come for her, she would be his bride. Then, a new bridal feast would be set for the wedding. In the meantime, Rhiannon planned with Powell to get out of the trouble. For this purpose, she gave him a magical bag, which he was to use when the right time should come.

Quickly the twelve months passed and then Gwawl appeared again, to claim his bride, and a great feast was spread in his honour. All were having a good time, when in the midst of their merriment, a beggar appeared in the hall. He was in rags and carried the usual beggar's wallet for food or alms. He asked only that, out of the abundance on the table, his bag might be filled. Gwawl agreed and ordered his servants to attend to the matter.

But the bag never got full. What they put into it, or how much made no difference. Dish after dish was emptied. By degrees, most of the food on the table was in the beggar's bag.

"My soul alive! Will that bag never get full?" asked Gwawl.

"No, by Heaven! Not unless some rich man shall get into it, stamp it down with his feet, and call out 'enough.'"

Then Rhiannon, who sat beside Gwawl, urged him to attempt the task, by putting his two feet in the bag to stamp it down. No sooner had Gwawl done this, than the supposed beggar pushed him down inside the bag. Then drawing the mouth shut, he tied it tight over Gwawl's head.

Then the beggar's rags dropped, and there stood forth the handsome leader, Powell. He blew his horn, and in rushed his knights who overcame and bound the followers of Gwawl. Then they proceeded to play a merry game of football, using the bag, in which Gwawl was tied, as men in our day kick pigskin. One called to his mate, or rival, "What's in the bag?" and others answered, "a badger." So, they played the game of "Badger in the Bag," kicking it around the hall.

They did not let the prisoner out of the bag, until he had promised to pay the pipers, the harpers, and the singers, who should come to the wedding of Powell and Rhiannon. He must give up all his claims and register a vow never to take revenge. This oath given, and promises made, the bag was opened, and the agreements solemnly confirmed in presence of all. Then Gwawl, and every one of his men, knights and servants, were let go, and they went back to their own country.

A few evenings later, in the large banqueting hall, Powell and Rhiannon were married. Besides the great feast, presents were given to all present, high and low. Then the happy pair made their wedding journey to Gwawl's palace at Narberth. There the lovely bride gave a ring, or a gem, to every lord and lady in her new realm, and everybody was happy.

ROBERT ROBERTS AND THE FAIRIES

Adapted from Fairy-Tales & Other Stories by Peter Henry Emerson, published by D. Nutt, London in 1894.

ROBERT ROBERTS WAS A CARPENTER WHO worked hard and well; but he could never keep his tongue still. One day, as he was crossing a brook, a little man came up to him and said:

"Robert Roberts, go up to the holly tree that leans over the road on the Red-hill, and dig below it, and you shall be rewarded."

The very next morning, at daybreak, Robert Roberts set out for the spot, and dug a great hole, before anyone was up, when he found a box of gold. He went to the same place twice afterwards, and dug, and found gold each time. But as he grew rich, he began to boast and hint that he had mysterious friends. One day, when the talk turned on the fairies, he said that he knew them right well, and that they gave him money. Robert Roberts thought no more of the matter until he went to the spot a week afterwards, one evening at dusk. When he got to the tree, and began to dig as usual, big stones came rolling down the bank, just missing him, so that he ran for his life, and never went near the place again.

ROWLI PUGH

Adapted from British Goblins - Welsh Folk-lore, Fairy Mythology,
Legends and Traditions by Wirt Sikes, United States Consul for
Wales. Published by Sampson Low, Marston, Searle & Rivington
in 1880

ON A CERTAIN FARM IN GLAMORGANSHIRE lived Rowli Pugh, who was known far and wide for his evil luck. Nothing prospered that he turned his hand to; his crops proved poor, though his neighbours' might be good; his roof leaked in spite of all his mending; his walls remained damp when everyone else's walls were dry; and above all, his wife was so feeble she could do no work. His fortunes at last seemed so hard that he resolved to sell out and clear out, no matter at what loss, and try to better himself in another country.

So as Rowli was sitting on his wall one day, hard by his cottage, musing over his sad lot, he was accosted by a little man who asked him what the matter was. Rowli looked around in surprise, but before he could answer the ellyll said to him with a grin, "There, there, hold your tongue, I know more about you than you ever dreamed of knowing. You're in trouble, and you're going away. But you may stay, now I've spoken to you. Only bid your good wife leave the candle burning when she goes to bed and say no more about it."

With this the ellyll kicked up his heels and disappeared. Of course, the farmer did as he was bid, and from that day he prospered. Every night Catti Jones, his wife, set the candle out, swept the hearth, and went to bed; and every night the fairies would come and do her baking and brewing, her washing and mending, sometimes even furnishing their own tools and materials. The farmer was now always clean of linen and whole of garb; he had good bread and good beer; he felt like a new man and worked like one.

Everything prospered with him now as nothing had before. His crops were good, his barns were tidy, his cattle were sleek, his pigs the fattest in the parish. So, things went on for three years. One night Catti Jones took it into her head that she must have a peep at the fair family who did her work for her; and curiosity conquering prudence, she arose while Rowli Pugh lay snoring, and peeped through a crack in the door.

There they were, a jolly company of ellyllon, working away like mad, and laughing and dancing as madly as they worked. Catti was so amused that in spite of herself she fell to laughing too; and at sound of her voice the ellyllon scattered like mist before the wind, leaving the room empty. They never came back any more; but the farmer was now prosperous, and his bad luck never returned to plague him.

TAFFY AP SION

Adapted from British Goblins - Welsh Folk-lore, Fairy Mythology,
Legends and Traditions by Wirt Sikes, United States Consul for
Wales. Published by Sampson Low, Marston, Searle & Rivington
in 1880

TAFFY AP SION, THE SHOEMAKER'S SON, living near
Pencader, Carmarthenshire, was a lad who many years ago entered
the fairy circle on the mountain hard by there, and having danced a
few minutes, as he supposed, chanced to step out. He was then
astonished to find that the scene which had been so familiar was
now quite strange to him. Here were roads and houses he had never
seen, and in place of his father's humble cottage there now stood a
fine stone farm-house. About him were lovely cultivated fields
instead of the barren mountain he was accustomed to.

"Ah," thought he, "this is some fairy trick to deceive my eyes. It is
not ten minutes since I stepped into that circle, and now when I
step out they have built my father a new house! Well, I only hope it
is real; anyhow, I'll go and see."

So, he started off by a path he knew instinctively, and suddenly
struck against a very solid hedge. He rubbed his eyes, felt the
hedge with his fingers, scratched his head, felt the hedge again, ran
a thorn into his fingers and cried out, "Ow! This is no fairy hedge

anyhow, nor, from the age of the thorns, was it grown in a few minutes" time."

So he climbed over it and walked on. "Here was I born," said he, as he entered the farmyard, staring wildly about him, "and not a thing here do I know!" His mystification was complete when there came bounding towards him a huge dog, barking furiously. "What dog is this? Get out, you ugly brute! Don't you know I'm master here? At least, when mothers from home, for father don't count." But the dog only barked the harder.

"Surely," muttered Taffy to himself, "I have lost my road and am wandering through some unknown neighbourhood; but no, yonder is the Careg Hir!" and he stood staring at the well-known erect stone thus called, which still stands on the mountain south of Pencader, and is supposed to have been placed there in ancient times to commemorate a victory. As Taffy stood thus looking at the Long Stone, he heard footsteps behind him, and turning, beheld the occupant of the farm-house, who had come out to see why his dog was barking.

Poor Taffy was so ragged and wan that the farmer's Welsh heart was at once stirred to sympathy. "Who are you, poor man?" he asked. To which Taffy answered, "I know who I was, but I do not know who I am now. I was the son of a shoemaker who lived in this place, this morning; for that rock, though it is changed a little, I know too well."

"Poor fellow," said the farmer, "you have lost your senses. This house was built by my great-grandfather, repaired by my grandfather; and that part there, which seems newly built, was done about three years ago at my expense. You must be deranged or have missed the road; but come in and refresh yourself with some victuals, and rest."

Taffy was half persuaded that he had overslept himself and lost his road, but looking back he saw the rock before mentioned, and exclaimed, "It is but an hour since I was on yonder rock robbing a hawk's nest."

"Where have you been since?" asked the farmer. Taffy related his adventure. "Ah," exclaimed the farmer, "I see how it is. You have been with the fairies. Pray, who was your father?"

"Sion Evan y Crydd o Glanrhyd," was the answer.

"I never heard of such a man," said the farmer, shaking his head, "nor of such a place as Glanrhyd, either: but no matter, after you have taken a little food we will step down to Catti Shon, at Pencader, who will probably be able to tell us something." With this he beckoned Taffy to follow him and walked on; but hearing behind him the sound of footsteps growing weaker and weaker, he turned around, when to his horror he beheld the poor fellow crumble in an instant to about a thimbleful of black ashes.

The farmer, though much terrified at this sight, preserved his calmness sufficiently to go at once and see old Catti, the aged crone he had referred to, who lived at Pencader, nearby. He found her crouching over a fire of faggots, trying to warm her old bones.

"And how do you do the day, Catti Shon?" asked the farmer. "Ah," said old Catti, "I'm wonderful well, farmer, considering how old I am." "Yes, yes, you're very old. Now, since you are so old, let me ask you something. Do you remember anything about Sion y Crydd o Glanrhyd? Was there ever such a man, do you know?"

"Sion Glanrhyd? O! I have some faint recollection of hearing my grandfather, old Evan Shenkin, Penferdir, relate that Sion's son was lost one morning, and they never heard of him afterwards, so that it was said he was taken by the fairies. His father's cot stood somewhere near your house."

"Were there many fairies about at that time?" asked the farmer.

"O yes; they were often seen on yonder hill, and I was told they were lately seen in Pant Shon Shenkin, eating flummery out of egg-shells, which they had stolen from a farm hard by."

"Dir anwyl fi!" cried the farmer; "dear me! I recollect now - I saw them myself!"

THE BABY-FARMER

Adapted from Fairy-Tales & Other Stories by Peter Henry Emerson,
published by D. Nutt, London in 1894.

OLD KADDY WAS A BABY-FARMER, AND one day she went to the woods to gather sticks for her fire, and whilst she was gathering the sticks she found a piece of gold and took it home; but she never told anyone she had found the money, for she always pretended to be very poor.

But though she was so poor, she used to dress two of her children in fine clothes; but the others, whom she did not like, she kept in the filthiest rags.

One day a man knocked at her door and asked to see the children.

He sat down in her little room, and she went and brought the ragged little boy and girl, saying she was very poor, and couldn't afford to dress them better; for she had been careful to hide the well-dressed little boy and girl in a cockloft.

After the stranger had gone she went to the cockloft to look for her well-dressed favourites, but they had disappeared, and they were never seen afterwards, for they were turned into fairies.

THE BLACK GREYHOUND

Adapted from Welsh Folk-Lore by Owain Elias, published in 1896
by Woodall, Minshall and Co, and based on Elias' prize essay of
the national Eisteddfod, 1887.

AN OLD WOMAN, CREDITED TO BE a witch, lived on the confines of the hills in a small hut in south Caernarvonshire. Her grandson, a sharp intelligent lad, lived with her.

Many gentlemen came to that part with greyhounds for the purpose of coursing, and the lad's services were always in requisition, for he never failed in starting a hare, and whenever he did so he was rewarded with a shilling. But it was noticed that the greyhounds never caught the hare which the lad started. The sport was always good, the race long and exciting, but the hare never failed to elude her pursuers.

Scores of times this occurred, until at last the sportsmen consulted a wise man, who gave it as his opinion that this was no ordinary hare, but a witch, and, he said, "She can never be caught but by a black greyhound."

A dog of this colour was sought for far and near, and at last found and bought. Away to the hills the coursers went, believing that now the hare was theirs. They called at the cottage for the lad to accompany them and start the prey. He was as ready as ever to lead them to their sport. The hare was soon started, and off the dog was slipped and started after it. The hare bounded away as usual, but then the hare saw that her pursuer was a match for her in swiftness, and, notwithstanding the twistings and windings, the dog was soon close behind the distressed hare.

The race became more and more exciting, for hound and hare exerted themselves to their very utmost, and the chase became hot, and still hotter. The spectators shouted in their excitement - "Hei! ci du," ("Hi! black dog,") for the black greyhound was gaining on his victim.

"Hei! Mam, gu," ("Hi! grandmother, dear,") shouted the lad, forgetting in his trouble that his grandmother was in the form of a hare. His was the only encouraging voice uttered on behalf of the poor hunted hare, but his single voice was hardly heard amidst the shouts of the many.

The pursuit was long and hard, dog and hare gave signs of distress, but shouts of encouragement buoyed up the strength of the dog. The chase was evidently coming to a close, and the hare was approaching the spot whence it started.

One single heart was filled with dread and dismay at the failing strength of the hare, and from that heart came the words, "Hei! Mam gu" ("Hi! grandmother, dear.")

Everyone followed the chase, which was now nearing the old woman's cottage, the window of which was open. With a bound the hare jumped through the small casement into the cottage, but the black dog was close behind her, and just as she was disappearing through the window, he bit the hare and retained a piece of her skin in his mouth. He could, not, of course, follow the hare into the cottage, as the aperture was too small.

The sportsmen lost no time in getting into the cottage, but, after much searching, they failed to discover the hare. All that they saw was an old woman seated by the fire spinning her yarn. They also noticed that there was blood trickling from underneath her seat, and this they considered sufficient proof that it was the witch in the form of a hare that had been coursed and had been bitten by the dog just as she bounded into the cottage.

THE BOY THAT WAS NAMED TROUBLE

Adapted from Welsh Fairy Tales by William Elliot Griffis and originally published in 1921.

IN ONE OF THE MANY "CO-EDS", or places with this name, in ancient and forest-covered Wales, there was a man who had one of the most beautiful mares in all the world. Yet great misfortunes befell both this Co-ed mare and her owner.

Every night, on the first of May, the mare gave birth to a pretty little colt. Yet no one ever saw, or could ever tell what became of any one, or all of the colts. Each and all, and one by one, they disappeared. Nobody knew where they were, or went, or what had become of them.

At last, the owner, who had no children, and loved little horses, determined not to lose another. He girded on his sword, and with his trusty spear, stood guard all night in the stable to catch the mortal robber, as he supposed he must be.

When on this same night of May first, the mare foaled again, and the colt stood up on its long legs, the man greatly admired the young creature. It looked already, as if it could, with its own legs, run away and escape from any wolf that should chase it, hoping to eat it up.

But at this moment, a great noise was heard outside the stable. The next moment a long arm, with a claw at the end of it, was poked through the window-hole, to seize the colt. Instantly the man drew his sword and with one blow, the claw part of the arm was cut off, and it dropped inside, with the colt.

Hearing a great cry and tumult outside, the owner of the mare rushed forth into the darkness. But though he heard howls of pain, he could see nothing, so he returned to the stable. There, at the door, he found a baby, with hair as yellow as gold, smiling at him. Besides its swaddling clothes, it was wrapped up in flame-coloured satin.

As it was still night, the man took the infant to his bed and laid it alongside of his wife, who was asleep. Now this good woman loved children, though she had none of her own, and so when she woke up in the morning, and saw what was beside her, she was very happy. Then she resolved to pretend that it was her own. So, she told her women, that she had borne the child, and they called him Gwri of the Golden Hair.

The boy baby grew up fast, and when only two years old, was as strong as most children are at six. Soon he was able to ride the colt that had been born on the May night, and the two were as playmates together.

Now it chanced, the man had heard the tale of Queen Rhiannon, wife of Powell, Prince of Dyfed. She had become the mother of a baby boy, but it was stolen from her at night. The six serving women, whose duty it was to attend to the Queen, and guard her child, were lazy and had neglected their duty. They were asleep when the baby was stolen away. To excuse themselves and be saved from punishment, they invented a lying story. They declared that Rhiannon had devoured the child, her own baby.

The wise men of the Court believed the story which the six wicked women had told, and Rhiannon, the Queen, though innocent, was condemned to do penance. She was to serve as a porter to carry visitors and their baggage from outdoors into the castle. Every day, for many months, through the hours of daylight, she stood in public disgrace in front of the castle of Narberth, at the stone block, on which riders on horses dismounted from the saddle. When anyone got off at the gate, she had to carry him or her on her back into the hall.

As the boy grew up, his foster father scanned his features closely, and it was not long before he made up his mind that Powell was his father and Rhiannon was his mother. One day, with the boy riding on his colt, and with two knights keeping him company, the owner of the Co-ed mare came near the castle of Narberth.

There they saw the beautiful Rhiannon sitting on the horse block at the gate. When they were about to dismount from their horses, the lovely woman spoke to them thus, "Chieftains, go no further thus. I will carry every one of you on my back, into the palace."

Seeing their looks of astonishment, she explained, "This is my penance for the charge brought against me of slaying my son and devouring him."

One and all the four refused to be carried and went into the castle on their own feet. There Powell, the prince, welcomed them and made a feast in their honour. It being night, Rhiannon sat beside him. After dinner when the time for story telling had come, the chief guest told the tale of his mare and the colt, and how he cut the clawed hand, and then found the boy on the doorstep.

Then to the joy and surprise of all, the owner of the Co-ed mare, putting the golden-haired boy before Rhiannon, cried out, "Behold lady, here is your son, and whoever they were who told the story and lied about your devouring your own child, have done you a grievous wrong."

Everyone at the table looked at the boy, and all recognized the lad at once as the child of Powell and Rhiannon.

"Here ends my pryderi (trouble)," cried out Rhiannon.

Thereupon one of the chiefs said, "Well have you named your child 'Trouble',"' and henceforth Pryderi was his name.

Soon it was made known, by the vision and word of the bards and seers, that all the mischief had been wrought by wicked fairies, and that the six serving women had been under their spell, when they lied about the Queen. Powell, the castle-lord, was so happy that he offered the man of Co-ed rich gifts of horses, jewels and dogs.

But this good man felt repaid in delivering a pure woman and loving mother from undeserved shame and disgrace, by wisdom and honesty according to common duty. As for Pryderi, he was educated as a king's son ought to be, in all gentle arts and was trained in all manly exercises.

After his father died, Pryderi became ruler of the realm. He married Kieva the daughter of a powerful chieftain, who had a pedigree as long as the bridle used to drive a ten-horse chariot. It reached back to Prince Casnar of Britain. Pryderi had many adventures, which are told in the Mabinogion, which is the great storehouse of Welsh hero, wonder, and fairy tales.

THE CORWRION CHANGELING LEGEND

Adapted from Welsh Folk-Lore by Owain Elias, published in 1896 by Woodall, Minshall and Co, and based on Elias' prize essay of the national Eisteddfod, 1887.

ONCE ON A TIME, IN THE fourteenth century, the wife of a man at Corwrion had twins, and she complained one day to the witch who lived close by, at Tyddyn y Barcut, that the children were not getting on, but that they were always crying, day and night.

"Are you sure that they are your children?" asked the witch, adding that it did not seem to her that they were like hers.

"I have my doubts also," said the mother.

"I wonder if somebody has changed children with you," said the witch.

"I do not know," said the mother.

"But why do you not seek to know?" asked the other.

"And how am I to go about it?" said the mother.

The witch replied, "Go and do something rather strange before their eyes and watch what they will say to one another."

"Well I do not know what I should do," said the mother.

"Oh,' said the witch, "take an egg-shell, and proceed to brew beer in it in a chamber aside and come here to tell me what the children will say about it."

The mother went home and did as the witch had directed her, and sure enough the two children lifted their heads out of the cradle to see what she was doing, to watch, and to listen. Then one observed to the other: "I remember seeing an oak having an acorn," to which the other replied, "And I remember seeing a hen having an egg," and one of the two added, "But I do not remember before seeing anybody brew beer in the shell of a hen's egg."

The mother then went to the witch and told her what the twins had said one to the other. The witch directed the mother to go to a small wooden bridge not far off, with one of the strange children under each arm, and there to drop them from the bridge into the river beneath.

The mother went back home again and did as she had been directed. When she reached home this time, to her astonishment, she found that her own children had been brought back.

THE CRAIG-Y-DON BLACKSMITH

Adapted from Fairy-Tales & Other Stories by Peter Henry Emerson,
published by D. Nutt, London in 1894.

ONCE UPON A TIME AN OLD blacksmith lived in an old forge at Craig-y-don, and he used to drink a great deal too much beer.

One night he was coming home from an alehouse very tipsy, and as he got near a small stream a lot of little men suddenly sprang up from the rocks, and one of them, who seemed to be older than the rest, came up to him, and said, "If you don't alter your ways of living you'll die soon; but if you behave better and become a better man you'll find it will be to your benefit," and they all disappeared as quickly as they had come.

The old blacksmith thought a good deal about what the fairies had told him, and he left off drinking, and became a sober, steady man.

One day, a few months after meeting the little people, a strange man brought a horse to be shod. Nobody knew either the horse or the man.

The old blacksmith tied the horse to a hole in the lip of a cauldron (used for the purpose of cooling his hot iron) that he had built in some masonry.

When he had tied the horse up he went to shoe the off hind-leg, but directly he touched the horse the spirited animal started back with a bound, and dragged the cauldron from the masonry, and then it broke the halter and ran away out of the forge and was never seen again: neither the horse nor its master.

When the old blacksmith came to pull down the masonry to rebuild it, he found three brass kettles full of money.

THE DREAM OF MAXEN WLEDIG

Taken originally from the Mabinogion and adapted here from Hero-Myths & Legends of the British Race by Maud Isabel Ebbutt, published by George G. Harrap & Co in 1910.

The Emperor Maxen Wledig

THE EMPEROR MAXEN WLEDIG WAS THE most powerful occupant of the throne of the Cæsars who had ever ruled Europe from the City of the Seven Hills. He was the most handsome man in his dominions, tall and strong and skilled in all manly exercises; withal he was gracious and friendly to all his vassals and tributary kings, so that he was universally beloved. One day he announced his wish to go hunting and was accompanied on his expedition down the Tiber valley by thirty-two vassal kings, with whom he enjoyed the sport heartily. At noon the heat was intense, they were far from Rome, and all were weary. The emperor proposed a halt, and they dismounted to take rest. Maxen lay down to sleep with his head on a shield, and soldiers and attendants stood around making a shelter for him from the sun's rays by a roof of shields hung on their spears. Thus, he fell into a sleep so deep that none dared to awake him.

Hours passed by, and still he slumbered, and still his whole retinue waited impatiently for his awakening. At length, when the evening shadows began to lie long and black on the ground, their impatience found vent in little restless movements of hounds chafing in their leashes, of spears clashing, of shields dropping from the weariness of their holders, and horses neighing and prancing; and then Maxen Wledig awoke suddenly with a start.

"Ah, why did you arouse me?" he asked sadly. "Lord, your dinner hour is long past. Did you not know?" they said. He shook his head mournfully, but said no word, and, mounting his horse, turned it and rode in unbroken silence back to Rome, with his head sunk on his breast. Behind him rode in dismay his retinue of kings and tributaries, who knew nothing of the cause of his sorrowful mood.

The Emperor's Malady

From that day the emperor was changed, changed utterly. He rode no more, he hunted no more, he paid no heed to the business of the empire but remained in seclusion in his own apartments and slept. The court banquets continued without him, music and song he refused to hear, and though in his sleep he smiled and was happy, when he awoke his melancholy could not be cheered or his gloom lightened. When this condition of things had continued for more than a week it was determined that the emperor must be aroused from this dreadful state of apathy, and his groom of the chamber, a noble Roman of very high rank, indeed, a king, under the emperor, resolved to make the endeavour.

"My lord," said he, "I have evil tidings for you. The people of Rome are beginning to murmur against you, because of the change that has come over you. They say that you are bewitched, that they can get no answers or decisions from you, and all the affairs of the empire go to wrack and ruin while you sleep and take no heed. You have ceased to be their emperor, they say, and they will cease to be loyal to you."

The Dream of the Emperor

Then Maxen Wledig roused himself and said to the noble: "Call hither my wisest senators and councillors, and I will explain the cause of my melancholy, and perhaps they will be able to give me relief." Accordingly, the senators came together, and the emperor ascended his throne, looking so mournful that the whole Senate grieved for him, and feared lest death should speedily overtake him.

He began to address them thus: "Senators and Sages of Rome, I have heard that my people murmur against me, and will rebel if I do not arouse myself. A terrible fate has fallen upon me, and I see no way of escape from my misery, unless ye can find one. It is now more than a week since I went hunting with my court, and when I was wearied I dismounted and slept. In my sleep I dreamt, and a vision cast its spell upon me, so that I feel no happiness unless I am sleeping and seem to live only in my dreams.

"I thought I was hunting along the Tiber valley, lost my courtiers, and rode to the head of the valley alone. There the river flowed forth from a great mountain, which looked to me the highest in the world; but I ascended it, and found beyond fair and fertile plains, far vaster than any in our Italy, with mighty rivers flowing through the lovely country to the sea. I followed the course of the greatest river, and reached its mouth, where a noble port stood on the shores of a sea unknown to me.

"In the harbour lay a fleet of well-appointed ships, and one of these was most beautifully adorned, its planks covered with gold or silver, and its sails of silk. As a gangway of carved ivory led to the deck, I crossed it and entered the vessel, which immediately sailed out of the harbour into the ocean.

"The voyage was not of long duration, for we soon came to land in a wondrously beautiful island, with scenery of varied loveliness. This island I traversed, led by some secret guidance, till I reached its farthest shore, broken by cliffs and precipices and mountain ranges, while between the mountains and the sea I saw a fair and fruitful land traversed by a silvery, winding river, with a castle at its mouth.

"My longing drew me to the castle, and when I came to the gate I entered, for the dwelling stood open to every man, and such a hall as was therein I have never seen for splendour, even in Imperial Rome. The walls were covered with gold, set with precious gems, the seats were of gold and the tables of silver, and two fair youths, whom I saw playing chess, used pieces of gold on a board of silver. Their attire was of black satin embroidered with gold, and golden circlets were on their brows.

"I gazed at the youths for a moment, and next became aware of an aged man sitting near them. His carved ivory seat was adorned with golden eagles, the token of Imperial Rome; his ornaments on arms and hands and neck were of bright gold, and he was carving fresh chessmen from a rod of solid gold. Beside him sat, on a golden chair, a maiden (the loveliest in the whole world she seemed, and still seems, to me). White was her inner dress under a golden overdress, her crown of gold adorned with rubies and pearls, and a golden girdle encircled her slender waist.

"The beauty of her face won my love in that moment, and I knelt and said: 'Hail, Empress of Rome!' but as she bent forward from her seat to greet me I awoke. Now I have no peace and no joy except in sleep, for in dreams I always see my lady, and in dreams we love each other and are happy; therefore, in dreams will I live, unless ye can find some way to satisfy my longing while I wake."

The Quest for the Maiden

The senators were at first greatly amazed, and then one of them said, "My lord, will you not send out messengers to seek throughout all your lands for the maiden in the castle? Let each group of messengers search for one year and return at the end of the year with tidings. So, shall you live in good hope of success from year to year."

The messengers were sent out accordingly, with wands in their hands and a sleeve tied on each cap, in token of peace and of an embassy; but though they searched with all diligence, after three years three separate embassies had brought back no news of the mysterious land and the beauteous maiden.

Then the groom of the chamber said to Maxen Wledig: "My lord, will you not go forth to hunt, as on the day when you dreamt this enthralling dream?" To this the emperor agreed and rode to the place in the valley where he had slept. "Here," he said, "my dream began, and I seemed to follow the river to its source."

Then the groom of the chamber said, "Will you not send messengers to the river's source, my lord, and bid them follow the track of your dream?" Accordingly, thirteen messengers were sent, who followed the river up until it issued from the highest mountain they had ever seen. "Behold our emperor's dream!" they exclaimed, and they ascended the mountain, and descended the other side into a most beautiful and fertile plain, as Maxen Wledig had seen in his dream.

Following the greatest river of all (probably the Rhine), the ambassadors reached the great seaport on the North Sea, and found the fleet waiting with one vessel larger than all the others; and they entered the ship and were carried to the fair island of Britain. Here they journeyed westward, and came to the mountainous land of Snowdon, whence they could see the sacred isle of Mona (Anglesey) and the fertile land of Arvon lying between the mountains and the sea. "This," said the messengers, "is the land of our master's dream, and in yon fair castle we shall find the maiden whom our emperor loves."

The Finding of the Maiden

So they went through the lovely land of Arvon to the castle of Caernarvon, and in that lordly fortress was the great hall, with the two youths playing chess, the venerable man carving chessmen, and the maiden in her chair of gold. When the ambassadors saw the fair Princess Helena they fell on their knees before her and said, "Empress of Rome, all hail!" But Helena half rose from her seat in anger as she said, "What does this mockery mean? You seem to be men of gentle breeding, and you wear the badge of messengers: whence comes it, then, that ye mock me thus?"

But the ambassadors calmed her anger, saying: "Be not angry, lady: this is no mockery, for the Emperor of Rome, the great lord Maxen Wledig, has seen you in a dream, and he has sworn to wed none but you. Which, therefore, will you choose, to accompany us to Rome, and there be made empress, or to wait here until the emperor can come to you?" The princess thought deeply for a time, and then replied: "I would not be too credulous, or too hard of belief. If the emperor loves me and would wed me, let him find me in my father's house, and make me his bride in my own home."

The Dream Realized

After this the thirteen envoys departed and returned to the emperor in such haste that when their horses failed they gave no heed but took others and pressed on. When they reached Rome and informed Maxen Wledig of the success of their mission he at once gathered his army and marched across Europe towards Britain.

When the Roman emperor had crossed the sea, he conquered Britain from Beli the son of Manogan, and made his way to Arvon. On entering the castle, he saw first the two youths, Kynon and Adeon, playing chess, then their father, Eudav, the son of Caradoc, and then his beloved, the beauteous Helena, daughter of Eudav.

"Empress of Rome, all hail!" Maxen Wledig said, and the princess bent forward in her chair and kissed him, for she knew he was her destined husband. The next day they were wedded, and the Emperor Maxen Wledig gave Helena as dowry all Britain for her father, the son of the gallant Caradoc, and for herself three castles, Caernarfon, Caerleon, and Carmarthen, where she dwelt in turn; and in one of them was born her son Constantine, the only British-born Emperor of Rome. To this day in Wales the old Roman roads that connected Helena's three castles are known as "Sarn Helen."

THE EGG SHELL POTTAGE

Adapted from Welsh Folk-Lore by Owain Elias, published in 1896 by Woodall, Minshall and Co, and based on Elias' prize essay of the national Eisteddfod, 1887.

IN THE PARISH OF TREFEGLWYS, NEAR Llanidloes, in the county of Montgomery, there is a little shepherd's cot, that is commonly called Twt y Cwmrws (The Place of Strife) on account of the extraordinary trouble that has occurred there. The inhabitants of the cottage were a man and his wife, and they had born to them twins, whom the woman nursed with great care and tenderness.

Some months afterwards indispensable business called the wife to the house of one of her nearest neighbours; yet, notwithstanding she had not far to go, she did not like to leave her children by themselves in their cradle, even for a minute, as her house was solitary, and there were many tales of goblins or the 'Tylwyth Têg' (the Fair Family or the Fairies) haunting the neighbourhood. However, she went, and returned as soon as she could; but on coming back she felt herself not a little terrified on seeing on her way, though it was mid-day, some of 'the old elves of the blue petticoat,' as they are usually called. However, when she got back to her house she was rejoiced to find everything in the state that she had left it.

But after some time had passed by, the good people began to wonder that the twins did not grow at all, but still remained small and childlike in stature. The man would have it that they were not his children; the woman said that they must be their children, and about this arose the great strife between them that gave name to the place where they lived.

One evening when the woman was very heavy of heart she determined to go and consult a Gwr Cyfarwydd, a local Wise Man, feeling assured that everything was known to him, and he gave her this counsel. Now there was to be a harvest soon of the rye and oats; so, the wise man offered this advice.

"When you are preparing dinner for the reapers empty the shell of a hen's egg and boil the shell full of pottage and take it out through the door as if you meant it for a dinner to the reapers, and then listen to what the twins will say. If you hear the children speaking things above the understanding of children, return into the house, take them, and throw them into the waves of Llyn Ebyr, which is very near to you. But if you don't hear anything remarkable, do them no injury.'

So, when the day of the reaping came the woman did all that the Gwr Cyfarwydd ordered and put the eggshell on the fire and took it off and carried it to the door, and there she stood and listened. Then she heard one of the children say to the other child:

Acorns before oak I knew,

An egg before a hen,

Never one hen's egg-shell stew

Enough for harvestmen!

On this the mother returned to her house and took the two children, and threw them into the Llyn, and suddenly the goblins in their trousers came to save the dwarves that they had left in the children's stead, and the woman had her own children back again, and thus the strife between her and her husband ended.

THE FAIRIES OF CARAGONAN

Adapted from Fairy-Tales & Other Stories by Peter Henry Emerson,
published by D. Nutt, London in 1894.

ONCE UPON A TIME A LOT of fairies lived in Mona. One day the queen fairy's daughter, who was now fifteen years of age, told her mother she wished to go out and see the world. The queen consented, allowing her to go for a day, and to change from a fairy to a bird, or from a bird to a fairy, as she wished.

When the young fairy returned one night she said, "I've been to a gentleman's house, and as I stood listening, I heard the gentleman was witched. He was very ill and crying out with pain."

"Oh, I must look into that," said the queen.

So, the next day she too disguised herself and found that he was bewitched by an old witch. So, the following day she set out with six other fairies, and when they came to the gentleman's house she found he was still gravely ill.

Going into the room, bearing a small blue pot they had brought with them, the queen asked the poorly gentleman, "Would you like to be cured?"

"Oh, bless you; yes, indeed," he replied.

Whereupon the queen put the little blue pot of perfume on the centre of the table, and lit it, when the room was instantly filled with the most delicious odour. Whilst the perfume was burning, the six fairies formed in line behind her, and she leading, they walked round the table three times, chanting in chorus:

"Round and round three times three,

We have come to cure thee."

At the end of the third round she touched the burning perfume with her wand, and then touched the gentleman on the head, saying, "Be you made whole."

No sooner had she said the words than he jumped up hale and hearty, and said, "Oh, dear queen, what shall I do for you? I'll do anything you wish."

"Money I do not wish for," said the queen, "but there's a little plot of ground on the sea-cliff I want you to lend me, for I wish to make a ring there, and the grass will die when I make the ring. Then I want you to build three walls round the ring, but leave the sea-side open, so that we may be able to come and go easily."

"With the greatest of pleasure," said the gentleman; and he built the three stone walls at once, at the spot indicated.

Near the gentleman lived the old witch, and she had the power of turning at will into a hare. The gentleman was a great hare hunter, but the hounds could never catch this hare, and it always disappeared into a mill, running between the wings and jumping in at an open window, though they stationed two men and a dog at the spot, when it immediately turned into the old witch. And the old miller never suspected, for the old woman used to take him a peck of corn to grind a few days before any hunt, telling him she would call for it on the afternoon of the day of the hunt. So that when she arrived she was expected.

One day she had been taunting the gentleman as he returned from a hunt, that he could never catch the hare, and he struck her with his whip, saying "Get away, you witchcraft!" Whereupon she witched him, and he fell ill, and was cured as we have seen.

When this gentleman got well he watched the old witch, and saw she often visited the house of an old miser who lived nearby with his beautiful niece. Now all the people in the village touched their hats most respectfully to this old miser, for they knew he had dealings with the witch, and they were as much afraid of him as of her; but everyone loved the miser's kind and beautiful niece.

When the fairies got home the queen told her daughter, "I have no power over the old witch for twelve months from today, and then I have no power over her life. She must lose that by the arm of a man."

So, the next day the daughter was sent out again to see whether she could find a person suited to that purpose. In the village lived a small crofter, who was afraid of nothing; he was the boldest man thereabouts; and one day he passed the miser without saluting him. The old fellow went off at once and told the witch.

"Oh, I'll settle his cows tonight!" said she, and they were taken sick, and gave no milk that night.

The fairy's daughter arrived at his croft-yard after the cows were taken ill, and she heard him say to his son, a bright lad, "It must be the old witch!"

When she heard this, she sent him to the queen, and so next day the fairy queen took six fairies and went to the croft, taking her blue pot of perfume. When she got there she asked the crofter if he would like his cows cured?

"God bless you, yes!" he said.

The queen made him bring a round table into the yard, whereon she placed the blue pot of perfume, and having lit it, as before, they formed in line and walked round thrice, chanting those same words.

"Round and round three times three,

We have come to cure thee."

Then she dipped the end of her wand into the perfume, and touched the cows on the forehead, saying to each one, "Be you whole." Whereupon they jumped up cured.

The little farmer was overjoyed, and cried, "Oh, what can I do for you? What can I do for you?"

"Money I care not for," said the queen, "all I want is your son to avenge you and me."

The lad jumped up and said, "What I can do I'll do it for you, my lady fairy."

She told him to be at the walled plot the following day at noon and left.

The next day at noon, the queen and her daughter and three hundred other fairies came up the cliff to the green grass plot, and they carried a pole, and a tape, and a mirror. When they reached the plot, they planted the pole in the ground, and hung the mirror on the pole. The queen took the tape, which measured ten yards and was fastened to the top of the pole, and walked round in a circle, and wherever she set her feet the grass withered and died. Then the fairies followed up behind the queen, and each fairy carried a harebell in her left-hand, and a little blue cup of burning perfume in her right. When they had formed up the queen called the lad to her side and told him to walk by her throughout. They then started off, all singing in chorus:

"Round and round three times three,

Tell me what you see."

When they finished the first round, the queen and lad stopped before the mirror, and she asked the lad what he saw?

"I see, I see, the mirror tells me,

it is the witch that I see,"

So, they marched round again, singing the same words as before, and when they stopped a second time before the mirror the queen again asked him what he saw?

"I see, I see, the mirror tells me,

It is a hare that I see,"

A third time the ceremony and question were repeated.

"I see, I see, the mirror tells me,

The hares run up the hill to the mill."

"Now," said the queen, "there is to be a hare-hunting this day week; be at the mill at noon, and I will meet you there." And then the fairies, pole, mirror, and all, vanished and only the empty ring on the green was left.

Upon the appointed day the lad went to his tryst, and at noon the Fairy Queen appeared, and gave him a sling, and a smooth pebble from the beach, saying, "I have blessed your arms, and I have blessed the sling and the stone. Then she sang softly:

"Now as the clock strikes three,

Go up the hill near the mill,

And in the ring stand still

Till you hear the click of the mill.

Then with your arm, with power and might,

You shall strike and smite

The devil of a witch called Jezebel light,

And you shall see an awful sight."

The lad did as he was bidden, and presently he heard the huntsman's horn and the hue and cry, and saw the hare running down the opposite hillside, where the hounds seemed to gain on her, but as she breasted the hill on which he stood she gained on them. As she came towards the mill he threw his stone, and it lodged in her skull, and when he ran up he found he had killed the old witch. As the huntsmen came up they crowded round him and praised him; and then they fastened the witch's body to a horse by ropes, and dragged her to the bottom of the valley, where they buried her in a ditch. That night, when the miser heard of her death, he dropped down dead on the spot.

As the lad was going home the queen appeared to him and told him to be at the ring the following day at noon.

Next day all the fairies came with the pole and mirror, each carrying a harebell in her left-hand, and a blue cup of burning perfume in her right, and they formed up as before, the lad walking beside the queen. They marched round and repeated the old words, when the queen stopped before the mirror, and said, "What do you see?"

"I see, I see, the mirror tells me,

It is an old plate-cupboard that I see."

A second time they went around, and the question, was repeated.

"I see, I see, the mirror tells me,
The back is turned to me."

A third time was the ceremony fulfilled, and the lad answered

"I see, I see, the mirror tells me,
A spring-door is open to me."

"Buy that plate-cupboard at the miser's sale," said the queen, and she and her companions disappeared as before.

Upon the day of the sale all the things were brought out in the road, and the plate-cupboard was put up, the lad recognising it and bidding up for it till it was sold to him. When he had paid for it he took it home in a cart, and when he got in and examined it, he found the secret drawer behind was full of gold. The following week the house and land, thirty acres, was put up for sale, and the lad bought both, and married the miser's niece, and they lived happily till they died.

THE FAIRIES' MINT

Adapted from Fairy-Tales & Other Stories by Peter Henry Emerson,
published by D. Nutt, London in 1894.

ONCE UPON A TIME THERE WAS a miller, who lived in Anglesey. One day he noticed that some of his sacks had been moved during the night. The following day he felt sure that some of his grain had been disturbed, and, lastly, he was sure someone had been working his mill in the night during his absence.

He confided his suspicions to a friend, and they determined to go the next night and watch the mill. The following night, at about midnight, as they approached the mill, that stood on a bare stony hill, they were surprised to find the mill all lit up and at work, the great sails turning in the black night.

Creeping up softly to a small window, the miller looked in, and saw a crowd of little men carrying small bags and emptying them into the millstones. He could not see, however, what was in the bags, so he crept to another window, when he saw golden coins coming from the mill, from the place where the flour usually ran out.

Immediately the miller went to the mill door, and, putting his key into the lock, he unlocked the door; and as he did so the lights went out suddenly, and the mill stopped working. As he and his friend went into the dark mill they could hear sounds of people running about, but by the time they lit up the mill again there was nobody to be seen, but scattered all about the millstones and on the floor were cockle-shells.

After that, many persons who passed the mill at midnight said they saw the mill lit up and working; but the old miller left the fairies alone to coin their money.

THE FAIRY OF THE DELL

Adapted from Fairy-Tales & Other Stories by Peter Henry Emerson,
published by D. Nutt, London in 1894.

IN OLDEN TIMES FAIRIES WERE SENT to oppose the evil-doings of witches, and to destroy their power. About three hundred years ago a band of fairies, sixty in number, with their queen, called Queen of the Dell, came to Mona to oppose the evil works of a celebrated witch. The fairies settled by a spring, in a valley. After having blessed the spring, or "well", as they called it, they built a bower just above the spring for the queen, placing a throne therein. Nearby they built a large bower for themselves to live in.

After that, the queen drew three circles, one within the other, on a nice flat grassy place by the well. When they were comfortably settled, the queen sent the fairies about the country to gather tidings of the people. They went from house to house, and everywhere heard great complaints against an old witch; how she had made some blind, others lame, and deformed others by causing a horn to grow out of their foreheads. When they got back to the well and told the queen. The Queen said, "I must do something for these old people, and though the witch is very powerful, we must break her power." So, the next day the queen fairy sent word to all the bewitched to congregate upon a fixed day at the sacred well, just before noon.

151

When the day came, several ailing people collected at the well. The queen then placed the patients in pairs in the inner ring, and the sixty fairies in pairs in the middle ring. Each little fairy was three feet and a half high, and carried a small wand in her right hand, and a bunch of fairy flowers, cuckoo's boots, baby's bells, and day's-eyes, in her left hand. Then the queen, who was four feet and a half in height, took the outside ring. On her head was a crown of wild flowers, in her right hand she carried a wand, and in her left a posy of fairy flowers. At a signal from the queen they began marching round the rings, singing in chorus:

"We march round by two and two

The circles of the sacred well

That lies in the dell."

When they had walked twice round the ring singing, the queen took her seat upon the throne, and calling each patient to her, she touched him with her wand and bade him go down to the sacred well and dip his body into the water three times, promising that all his ills should be cured. As each one came forth from the spring he knelt before the queen, and she blessed him, and told him to hurry home and put on dry clothes. So that all were cured of their ills.

Now the old witch who had worked all these evils lived near the well in a cottage. She had first learned witchcraft from a book called The Black Art, which a gentleman farmer had lent her when a girl. She progressed rapidly with her studies, and being eager to learn more, sold herself to the devil, who made compact with her that she should have full power for seven years, after which she was to become his. He gave her a wand that had the magic power of drawing people to her, and she had a ring on the grass by her house just like the fairy's ring. As the seven years were drawing to a close, and her heart was savage against the farmer who first led her into the paths of evil knowledge, she determined to be revenged. One day, soon after the Fairy of the Dell came to live by the spring, she drew the farmer to her with her wand, and, standing in her ring, she lured him into it. When he crossed the line, she said:

"Cursed be he or she

That crosses my circle to see me,"

She then touched him on the head and back, where a horn and a tail grew from the spots touched. He went off in a terrible rage, but she only laughed maliciously. But then, as she heard of the Queen of the Dell's good deeds, she repented of her evil deeds, and begged her neighbour to go to the queen fairy and ask her if she might come and visit her. The queen consented, and the old witch went down and told her everything about the book, of the magic wand, of the ring, and of all the wicked deeds she had done.

"O, you have been a bad witch," said the queen, "but I will see what I can do; but you must bring me the book and the wand;" and she told the old witch to come on the following day a little before noon. When the witch came the next day with her wand and book, she found the fairies had built a fire in the middle ring. The queen then took her and stood her by the fire, for she could not trust her on the outer circle.

"Now I must have more power," said the queen to the fairies, and she went and sat on the throne, leaving the witch by the fire in the middle ring. After thinking a little, the queen said, "Now I have it," and coming down from her throne muttering, she began walking round the outer circle, waiting for the hour of one o'clock, when all the fairies got into the middle circle and marched round, singing:

"At the hour of one
The cock shall crow one,
Goo! Goo! Goo!
I am here to tell
Of the sacred well
That lies in the dell,
And will conquer hell."

On the second round, they sang:

"At the hour of two
The cock crows two,
Goo! Goo! Goo!
I am here to tell
Of the sacred well
That lies in the dell;
We will conquer hell."

At the last round, they sang:

"At the hour of three

The cock crows three,

Goo! Goo! Goo!

I am here to tell

Of the sacred well

That lies in the dell;

Now I have conquered hell."

Then the queen cast the book and wand into the fire, and immediately the vale was rent by a thundering noise, and numbers of devils came from everywhere, and encircled the outer ring, but they could not pass the ring. Then the fairies began walking round and round, singing their song. When they had finished the song, they heard a loud screech from the devils that frightened all the fairies except the queen. She was unmoved, and going to the fire, stirred the ashes with her wand, and saw that the book and wand were burnt, and then she walked thrice round the outer ring by herself, when she turned to the devils, and said, "I command you to be gone from our earthly home, get to your own abode. I take the power of casting you all from here. Begone! begone! begone!" And all the devils flew up, and there was a mighty clap as of thunder, and the earth trembled, and the sky became overcast, and all the devils burst, and the sky cleared again.

After this the queen put three fairies by the old witch's side, and they constantly dipped their wands in the sacred spring, and touched her head, and she was sorely troubled and converted.

"Bring the mirror," said the queen.

And the fairies brought the mirror and laid it in the middle circle, and they all walked round three times, chanting again the song beginning "At the hour of one." When they had done this the queen stood still, and said, "Stand and watch to see what you can see." And as she looked she said:

"The mirror shines unto me

That the witch we can see

Has three devils inside of she."

Immediately the witch had a fit, and the three fairies had a hard job to keep the three devils quiet; indeed, they could not do so, and the queen had to go herself with her wand, for fear the devils should burst the witch asunder, and she said, "Come out three evil spirits, out of you."

And they came gnashing their teeth, and would have killed all the fairies, but the queen said, "Begone, begone, begone! you evil spirits, to the place of your abode," and suddenly the sky turned bright as fire, for the evil spirits were trying their spleen against the fairies, but the queen said, "Collect, collect, collect, into one fierce ball," and the fiery sky collected into one ball of fire more dazzling than the sun, so that none could look at it except the queen, who wore a black silk mask to protect her eyes. Suddenly the ball burst with a terrific noise, and the earth trembled.

"Enter into your abode, and never come down to our abode on earth anymore," said the queen.

And the witch was herself again, and she and the queen fairy were immediately great friends. The witch, when she came out of the ring, dropped on her knee and asked the queen if she might call her the Lady of the Dell, and how she could serve her.

"We will see about that," said the queen.

"Well, how do you live?" asked the woman who had been a witch.

"Well, I'll tell you," said the queen. "We go at midnight and milk the cows, and we keep the milk, and it never grows less so long as we leave some in the bottom of the vessel; we must not use it all. After milking the cow, we rub the cow's purse and bless it, and she gives double the amount of milk."

"Well, how do you get corn?"

"Well, we were at the mill playing one day, and the miller came in and saw us, and spoke kindly to us, and offered us some flour. 'We never take nothing for nothing,' I said, so I blessed the bin: so in a few minutes the bin was full to the brim with flour, and I said to the miller, 'Now don't you empty the bin, but always leave a peck in it, and for twelve months, no matter how much you use the bin, it will always be full in the morning.' Now I have told you this much, and I will tell further, 'You must love your neighbour, you must love all mankind.' Now here is a purse of gold, go and buy what you want, eggs, bacon, cheese, and get a flagon of wine and use these things freely, giving freely to the aged poor, and if you never finish these things, there will always be as much the next morning as you started with. And I shall make a salve for you, and you must use the water from the sacred well. That will be as a medicine, and people shall come from far and wide to be cured by you, and you shall be loved by all, and you shall be known to the poorest of the poor as Madame Dorothea."

And the woman did as she was told, and she became renowned for her medical skill, especially in childbirth, for her salve eased the pains, and her waters brought milk. By-and-by, she got known all over the island, and rich people came to her from afar, and she always made the rich pay, and the poor were treated free.

Madame Dorothea used to see the queen fairy at times, and one day she asked her, "Shall we meet again?"

"We cannot tell," said the queen, "but I will give you a ring. Let me place it on your finger. It is a magic ring worked by fairies. Whenever you seek to know of me, make a ring of your own, and walk round three times and rub the ring; if it turns bright I am alive, but if you see blood I am dead."

"But how can that be? You are much younger than I am."

"Oh, no! we fairies look young to the day of our death; we live to a great age, but die naturally of old age, for we never have any ailments, but still our power fades. Men fade in the flesh and power, but we fade only in power. I am over seventy now."

"But you look to be thirty."

"Well, we will shake hands and part, for I must go elsewhere; as I have no king, I do not stop in one place."

And they shook hands and parted.

THE FAIRY'S MIDWIFE

Adapted from Welsh Folk-Lore by Owain Elias, published in 1896 by Woodall, Minshall and Co, and based on Elias' prize essay of the national Eisteddfod, 1887.

A WELL-KNOWN MIDWIFE, WHOSE SERVICES WERE much sought after in consequence of her great skill, had one night retired to rest, when she was disturbed by a loud knocking at her door. She immediately got up and went to the door, and there saw a beautiful carriage, which she was urgently requested to enter at once to be conveyed to a house where her help was required. She did so, and after a long drive the carriage drew up before the entrance to a large mansion, which she had never seen before.

She successfully performed her work and stayed on in the place until her services were no longer required. Then she was conveyed home in the same manner as she had come, but with her went many valuable presents in grateful recognition of the services she had rendered.

The midwife somehow or other found out that she had been attending a Fairy mother. Sometime after her return from Fairy land she went to a fair, and there she saw the lady whom she had put to bed nimbly going from stall to stall and making many purchases.

For a while she watched the movements of the lady, and then presuming on her limited acquaintance, addressed her, and asked how she was. The lady seemed surprised and annoyed at the woman's speech, and instead of answering her, said, "And do you see me?"

"Yes, I do," said the midwife.

"With which eye?" enquired the Fairy.

"With this," said the woman, placing her hand on the eye.

No sooner had she spoken than the Fairy lady touched that eye, and the midwife could no longer see the Fairy.

THE GREAT RED DRAGON OF WALES

Adapted from Welsh Fairy Tales by William Elliot Griffis and originally published in 1921.

EVERY OLD COUNTRY THAT HAS WON fame in history and built up a civilization of its own, has a national flower. Besides this, some living creature, bird, or beast, or, it may be, a fish is on its flag. In places of honour, it stands as the emblem of the nation; that is, of the people, apart from the land they live on. Besides flag and symbol, it has a motto. That of Wales is: "Awake: It is light."

Now because the glorious stories of Wales, Scotland and Ireland have been nearly lost in that of mighty England, men have at times, almost forgotten about the leek, the thistle, and the shamrock, which stand for the other three divisions of the British Isles.

Yet each of these peoples has a history as noble as that of which the rose and the lion are the emblems. Each has also its patron saint and civilizer. So, we have Saint George, Saint David, Saint Andrew, and Saint Patrick, all of them white-souled heroes. On the union flag, or standard of the United Kingdom, we see their three crosses.

The lion of England, the harp of Ireland, the thistle of Scotland, and the Red Dragon of Wales represent the four peoples in the British Isles, each with its own speech, traditions, and emblems, yet all in unity and in loyalty, none excelling the Welsh, whose symbol is the Red Dragon. In classic phrase, we talk of Albion, Scotia, Cymry, and Hibernia.

But why red? Almost all the other dragons in the world are white, or yellow, green or purple, blue, or pink. Why a fiery red colour like that of Mars?

Borne on the banners of the Welsh archers, who in old days won the battles of Crecy and Agincourt, and now seen on the crests on the town halls and city flags, in heraldry, and in art, the red dragon is as rampant, as when King Arthur sat with His Knights at the Round Table.

The Red Dragon has four three-toed claws, a long, barbed tongue, and tail ending like an arrow head. With its wide wings unfolded, it guards those ancient liberties, which neither Saxon, nor Norman, nor German, nor kings on the throne, whether foolish or wise, have ever been able to take away. No people on earth combine so handsomely loyal freedom and the larger patriotism or hold in purer loyalty to the union of hearts and hands in the British Empire, which the sovereign represents, as do the Welsh.

The Welsh are the oldest of the British peoples. They preserve the language of the Druids, bards, and chiefs, of primeval ages which go back and far beyond any royal line in Europe, while most of their fairy tales are pre-ancient and beyond the dating. Why the Cymric dragon is red, is thus told, from times beyond human record:

It was in those early days, after the Romans in the south had left the island, and the Cymric king, Vortigern, was hard pressed by the Picts and Scots of the north. To his aid, he invited over from beyond the North Sea, or German Ocean, the tribes called the Long Knives, or Saxons, to help him. But once on the big island, these friends became enemies and would not go back. They wanted to possess all Britain.

Vortigern thought this was treachery. Knowing that the Long Knives would soon attack him, he called his twelve wise men together for their advice. With one voice, they advised him to retreat westward behind the mountains into Cymry. There he must build a strong fortress and there defy his enemies.

So the Saxons, who were Germans, thought they had driven the Cymry beyond the western borders of the country which was later called England, and into what they named the foreign or Welsh parts. Centuries afterwards, this land received the name of Wales.

The place chosen for the fortified city of the Cymry was among the mountains. From all over his realm, the King sent for masons and carpenters and collected the materials for building. Then, a solemn invocation was made to the gods by the Druid priests. These grand looking old men were robed in white, with long, snowy beards falling over their breasts, and they had milk-white oxen drawing their chariot. With a silver knife they cut the mistletoe from the tree-branch, hailing it as a sign of favour from God. Then with harp, music and song they dedicated the spot as a stronghold of the Cymric nation.

Then the King set the diggers to work. He promised a rich reward to those men of the pick and shovel who should dig the fastest and throw up the most dirt, so that the masons could, at the earliest moment, begin their part of the work.

But it all turned out differently from what the king expected. Some dragon, or powerful being underground, must have been offended by this invasion of his domain; for, the next morning, they saw that everything in the form of stone, timber, iron or tools, had disappeared during the night. It looked as if an earthquake had swallowed them all up.

Both king and seers, priests and bards, were greatly puzzled at this. However, not being able to account for it, and the Saxons likely to march on them at any time, the sovereign set the diggers at work and again collected more wood and stone. This time, even the women helped, not only to cook the food, but to drag the logs and stones. They were even ready to cut off their beautiful long hair to make ropes, if necessary. But in the morning, all had again disappeared, as if swept by a tempest. The ground was bare.

Nevertheless, all hands began again, for all hearts were united. For the third time, the work proceeded. Yet when the sun rose next morning, there was not even a trace of either material or labour. What was the matter? Had some dragon swallowed everything up?

Vortigern again summoned his twelve wise men, to meet in council, and to inquire concerning the cause of the marvel and to decide what was to be done. After long deliberation, while all the workmen and people outside waited for their verdict, the wise men agreed upon a remedy.

Now in ancient times, it was a custom, all over the world, notably in China and Japan and among our ancestors, that when a new castle or bridge was to be built, they sacrificed a human being. This was done either by walling up the victim while alive, or by mixing his or her blood with the cement used in the walls. Often it was a virgin, or a little child thus chosen by lot and made to die, the one for the many. The idea was not only to ward off the anger of the spirits of the air, or to appease the dragons underground, but also to make the workmen do their best work faithfully, so that the foundation should be sure, and the edifice withstand the storm, the wind, and the earthquake shocks.

So, nobody was surprised, or raised his eyebrows, or shook his head, or pursed up his lips, when the king announced that what the wise men declared, must be done and that quickly. Nevertheless, many a mother hugged her darling more closely to her bosom, and fathers feared for their sons or daughters, lest one of these, their own, should be chosen as the victim to be slain.

King Vortigern had the long horn blown for perfect silence, and then he spoke. "A child must be found who was born without a father. He must be brought here and be solemnly put to death. Then his blood will be sprinkled on the ground and the citadel will be built securely."

Within an hour, swift runners were seen bounding over the Cymric hills. They were dispatched in search of a boy without a father, and a large reward was promised to the young man who found what was wanted. So, into every part of the Cymric land, the searchers went.

One messenger noticed some boys playing ball. Two of them were quarrelling. Coming near, he heard one say to the other, "Oh, you boy without a father, nothing good will ever happen to you."

"This must be the one looked for," said the royal messenger to himself. So, he went up to the boy, who had been thus twitted and spoke to him, "Don't mind what he says." Then he prophesied great things, if he would go along with him. The boy was only too glad to go, and the next day the lad was brought before King Vortigern.

The workmen and their wives and children, numbering thousands, had assembled for the solemn ceremony of dedicating the ground by shedding the boy's blood. In strained attention the people held their breath.

The boy asked the king, "Why have your servants brought me to this place?" Then the sovereign told him the reason, and the boy asked, "Who instructed you to do this?"

"My wise men told me so to do, and even the sovereign of the land obeys his wise councillors."

"Order them to come to me, Your Majesty," pleaded the boy.

When the wise men appeared, the boy, in respectful manner, inquired of them thus, "How was the secret of my life revealed to you? Please speak freely and declare who it was that discovered me to you." Turning to the king, the boy added, "Pardon my boldness, Your Majesty. I shall soon reveal the whole matter to you, but I wish first to question your advisers. I want them to tell you what the real cause is, and reveal, if they can, what is hidden here underneath the ground."

But the wise men were confounded. They could not tell, and they fully confessed their ignorance.

The boy then said, "There is a pool of water down below. Please order your men to dig for it."

At once the spades were plied by strong hands, and in a few minutes the workmen saw their faces reflected, as in a looking glass. There was a pool of clear water there.

Turning to the wise men, the boy asked before all, "Now tell me, what is in the pool?"

As ignorant as before, and now thoroughly ashamed, the wise men were silent.

"Your Majesty, I can tell you, even if these men cannot. There are two vases in the pool."

Two brave men leaped down into the pool. They felt around and brought up two vases, as the boy had said.

Again, the lad put a question to the wise men, "What is in these vases?"

Once more, those who professed to know the secrets of the world, even to the demanding of the life of a human being, held their tongues.

"There is a tent in them," said the boy. "Separate them, and you will find it so."

By the king's command, a soldier thrust in his hand and found a folded tent. Again, while all wondered, the boy was in command of the situation. Everything seemed so reasonable, that all were prompt and alert to serve him.

"What a splendid chief and general, he would make, to lead us against our enemies, the 'Long Knives!'" whispered one soldier to another.

"What is in the tent?" asked the boy of the wise men.

Not one of the twelve knew what to say, and there was an almost painful silence.

"I will tell you, Your Majesty, and all here, what is in this tent. There are two serpents, one white and one red. Unfold the tent."

With such a leader, no soldier was afraid, nor did a single person in the crowd draw back? Two stalwart fellows stepped forward to open the tent. But now, a few of the men and many of the women shrank back while those that had babies, or little folks, snatched up their children, fearing lest the poisonous snakes might wriggle towards them. The two serpents were coiled up and asleep, but they soon showed signs of waking, and their fiery, lidless eyes glared at the people.

"Now, Your Majesty, and all here, be you the witnesses of what will happen. Let the King and wise men look in the tent."

At this moment, the serpents stretched themselves out at full length, while all fell back, giving them a wide circle to struggle in. Then they reared their heads. With their glittering eyes flashing fire, they began to struggle with each other. The white one rose up first, threw the red one into the middle of the arena, and then pursued him to the edge of the round space. Three times did the white serpent gain the victory over the red one. But while the white serpent seemed to be gloating over the other for a final onset, the red one, gathering strength, erected its head and struck at the other.

The struggle went on for several minutes, but in the end the red serpent overcame the white, driving it first out of the circle, then from the tent, and into the pool, where it disappeared, while the victorious red one moved into the tent again.

When the tent flap was opened for all to see, nothing was visible except a red dragon; for the victorious serpent had turned into this great creature which combined in one new form the body and the powers of bird, beast, reptile and fish. It had wings to fly, the strongest animal strength, and could crawl, swim, and live in either water or air, or on the earth. In its body was the sum total of all life.

Then, in the presence of all the assembly, the youth turned to the wise men to explain the meaning of what had happened. But not a word did they speak. In fact, their faces were full of shame before the great crowd.

"Now, Your Majesty, let me reveal to you the meaning of this mystery."

"Speak on," said the King, gratefully.

"This pool is the emblem of the world, and the tent is that of your kingdom. The two serpents are two dragons. The white serpent is the dragon of the Saxons, who now occupy several of the provinces and districts of Britain and from sea to sea. But when they invade our soil our people will finally drive them back and hold fast forever their beloved Cymric land. But you must choose another site, on which to erect your castle."

After this, whenever a castle was to be built no more human victims were doomed to death. All the twelve men, who had wanted to keep up the old cruel custom, were treated as deceivers of the people. By the King's orders, they were all put to death and buried before all the crowd.

Today, like so many who keep alive old and worn-out notions by means of deception and falsehood, these men are remembered only by the Twelve Mounds, which rise on the surface of the field hard by.

As for the boy, he became a great magician, or, as we in our age would call him, a man of science and wisdom, named Merlin. He lived long on the mountain, but when he went away with a friend, he placed all his treasures in a golden cauldron and hid them in a cave. He rolled a great stone over its mouth. Then with sod and earth he covered it all over so as to hide it from view. His purpose was to leave this his wealth for a leader, who, in some future generation, would use it for the benefit of his country, when most needed.

This special person will be a youth with yellow hair and blue eyes. When he comes to Denas, a bell will ring to invite him into the cave. The moment his foot is over the place, the stone of entrance will open of its own accord. Anyone else will be considered an intruder and it will not be possible for him to carry away the treasure.

THE HERON, THE CAT & THE BRAMBLE

Adapted from Welsh Folk-Lore by Owain Elias, published in 1896 by Woodall, Minshall and Co, and based on Elias' prize essay of the national Eisteddfod, 1887.

THE HERON AS IT FLIES SLOWLY towards the source of a river is said to be going up the river to bring the water down, in other words, this flight is a sign of coming rain. The same thing is said of the crane.

The heron, the cat, and the bramble bought the tithe of a certain parish. The heron bought the hay, mowed it, harvested it, and cocked it, and intended carrying it the following day, but in the night a storm came on, and carried the hay away, and ever since then the heron frequents the banks of the rivers and lakes, looking for her hay that was carried away, and saying "Pay me my tithe."

The cat bought the oats, cut them, and even threshed them, and left them in the barn, intending the following day to take them to the market for sale. But when she went into the barn, early the next morning, she found the floor covered with rats and mice, which had devoured the oats, and the cat flew at them and fought with them, and drove them from the barn, and this is why she is at enmity with rats and mice even to our day.

The bramble bought the wheat, and was more fortunate than the heron and cat, for the wheat was bagged, and taken to the market and sold, but sold on trust, and the bramble never got the money, and this is why it takes hold of everyone and says, "Pay me my tithe," for it forgot to whom the wheat had been sold.

THE HIDDEN GOLDEN CHAIR

Adapted from Welsh Folk-Lore by Owain Elias, published in 1896 by Woodall, Minshall and Co, and based on Elias' prize essay of the national Eisteddfod, 1887.

THERE WAS ONCE A BEAUTIFUL GIRL, the daughter of poor hard-working parents, who held a farm on the side of a hill, and their handsome industrious daughter took care of the sheep. At certain times of the year she visited the sheep-walk daily, but she never went to the mountain without her knitting needles, and when looking after the sheep she was always knitting stockings, and she was so clever with her needles that she could knit as she walked along.

The Fairies who lived in those mountains noticed this young woman's good qualities. One day, when she was far from home, watching her father's sheep, she saw before her a most beautiful golden chair. She went up to it and found that it was so massive that she could not move it. She knew the Fairy-lore of her neighbourhood, and she understood that the Fairies had, by revealing the chair, intended it for her, but there she was on the wild mountain, far away from home, without anyone near to assist her in carrying it away. And often had she heard that such treasures were to be taken possession of at once, or they would disappear forever.

She did not know what to do, but then she thought, if she could attach the yarn in her hand to the chair and then connect it with her home, the chair would be hers forever. Acting upon this thought she forthwith tied the yarn to the foot of the chair, and commenced unrolling the ball, walking the while homewards.

But long before she could reach her home the yarn in the ball was exhausted; she, however, tied it to the yarn in the stocking which she had been knitting, and again started towards her home, hoping to reach it before the yarn in the stocking would be finished. Sadly, the girl was doomed to disappointment, for that stocking yarn gave out before she could arrive at her father's house. She had nothing else with her to attach to the yarn.

She, however, could now see her home, and she began to shout, hoping to gain the ear of her parents, but no one appeared. In her distress she fastened the end of the yarn to a large stone and ran home as fast as she could. She told her parents what she had done, and all three proceeded immediately towards the stone to which the yarn had been tied, but they failed to discover it. The yarn, too, had disappeared. They continued a futile search for the golden chair until driven away by the approaching night.

The next day they renewed their search, but all in vain, for the girl was unable to find the spot where she had first seen the golden chair. It was believed by everybody that the Fairies had not only removed the golden chair, but also the yarn and stone to which the yarn had been attached, but people thought that if the yarn had been long enough to reach from the chair to the girl's home then the golden chair would have been hers forever.

Such is the tale. To this very day people still believe that the golden chair remains hidden away in the mountain, and that someday or other it will be given to those for whom it is intended. But it is, they say, no use anyone looking for it, as it is not to be got by searching, but it will be revealed, as if by accident, to those fated to possess it.

THE KING'S FOOT HOLDER

Adapted from Welsh Fairy Tales by William Elliot Griffis and originally published in 1921.

THERE WAS A CURIOUS CUSTOM IN the far olden times of Wales. At the banqueting hall, the king of the country would sit with his feet in the lap of a high officer. Whenever His Majesty sat down to dinner, this official person would be under the table holding the royal feet. This was also the case while all sat around the evening fire in the middle of the hall. This foot holding person was one of the king's staff and every castle must have a human footstool as part of its furniture.

By and by, it became the fashion for pretty maidens to seek this task, or to be chosen for the office. Their names in English sounded like Foot-Ease, Orthopede, or Foot Lights. When she was a plump and petite maid, they nicknamed her Twelve Inches, or when unusually soothing in her caresses of the soft royal toes. It was considered a high honour to be the King's Foot Holder. In after centuries, it was often boasted of that such and such an ancestor had held this honourable service.

One picture of castle life, as given in one of the old books tells how Kaim, the king's officer, went to the mead cellar with a golden cup, to get a drink that would keep them all wide awake. He also brought a handful of skewers on which they were to broil the collops, or bits of meat at the fire.

While they were doing this, the King sat on a seat of green rushes, over which was spread a flame-coloured satin cover, with a cushion like it, for his elbow to rest upon.

In the evening, the harpers and singers made music, the bards recited poetry, or the good storytellers told tales of heroes and wonders. During all this time, one or more maidens held the king's feet, or took turns at it, when tired; for often the revels or songs and tales lasted far into the night. At intervals, if the story was dull, or he had either too much dinner, or had been out hunting and got tired, His Majesty took a nap, with his feet resting upon the lap of a pretty maiden. This happened often in the late hours, while they were getting the liquid refreshments ready.

Then the king's chamberlain gently nudged him, to be wide awake, and he again enjoyed the music, and the stories, while his feet were held.

Now there was once a Prince of Gwynedd, in Wales, named Math, who was so fond of having his feet held, that he neglected to govern his people properly. He spent all his time lounging in an easy chair, while a pretty maiden held his heels and toes. He committed all public cares to two of his nephews. These were named for short, Gily and Gwyd.

The one whom the king loved best to have her hold his feet was the fairest maiden in all the land, and she was named Goewen. By and by, the prince grew so fond of having his feet held, and stroked and patted and played with, by Goewen, that he declared that he could not live, unless Goewen held his feet. And, she said, that if she did not hold the king's feet, she would die.

Now this Gily, one of the king's nephews, son of Don, whom he had appointed to look day by day after public affairs, would often be in the hall at night. He listened to the music and stories, and seeing Goewen, the king's foot holder, he fell in love with her. His eye usually wandered from the storyteller to the lovely girl holding the king's feet, and he thought her as beautiful as an angel.

Soon he became so lovesick, that he felt he would risk or give his life to get and have her for his own. But what would the king say? Besides, he soon found out that the maiden Goewen cared nothing for him.

Nevertheless, the passion of the lovelorn youth burned hotly and kept increasing. He confided his secret to his brother Gwyd, and asked his aid, which was promised. So, one day, the brother went to King Math, and begged for leave to go to Pryderi. In the king's name, he would ask from him the gift of a herd of swine of famous breed; which, in the quality of the pork they furnished, excelled all other pigs known. They were finer than any seen in the land, or ever heard of before. Their flesh was said to be sweeter, juicier, and more tender than the best beef. Even their manners were better than those of some men. In fact, these famous pigs were a present from the King of Fairyland. So highly were they prized, that King Math doubted much whether his nephew could get them at any price.

In ancient Wales the bards and poet singers were welcomed, and trusted above all men; and this, whether in the palace or the cottage. So Gwyd, the brother of the love-sick one, in order to get the herd of surpassing swine, took ten companions, all young men and strong, dressed as bards, and pretending by their actions to be such. Then they all started out together to seek the palace of Pryderi.

Having arrived, they were entertained at a great feast, in the castle hall. There Pryderi sat on his throne-chair, with his feet in a maiden's lap. The dinner over, Gwyd was asked to tell a story. This he did, delighting everyone so much, that he was voted a jolly good fellow by all. In fact, Pryderi felt ready to give him anything he might demand, excepting always his foot holder.

At once, Gwyd made request to give him the herd of swine.

At this, the countenance of Pryderi fell, for he had made a promise to his people, that he would not sell or give away the swine, until they had produced double their number in the land; for there were no pigs and no pork like theirs, to be bought anywhere.

Now this Gwyd was not very cunning, but he had the power of using magic arts. By these, he could draw the veil of illusion over both the mind and the eyes of the people. So, he made answer to Pryderi's objections thus: "Keep your promise to your people, oh, most honoured Pryderi, and only exchange them for the gift I make thee," said Gwyd.

Thereupon, exerting his powers of magic, he created the illusion of twelve superb horses. These were all saddled, bridled, and magnificently caparisoned. But, after twenty-four hours, they would vanish from sight. The illusion would be over.

With these steeds, so well fitted for hunting, were twelve sleek, fleet hounds. Taken altogether, here was a sight to make a hunter's eyes dance with delight. So Pryderi gave Gwyd the swine, and he quickly drove them off. "For," he whispered to his companion fellows in knavery, "the illusion will only last until the same hour tomorrow."

And so it happened. For when Pryderi's men went to the stables, to groom the horses and feed the hounds, there was nothing in either the stables or the kennels. When they told this to Pryderi, he at once blew his horn and assembled his knights, to invade the country of Gwynedd, to recover his swine. Hearing of his coming, King Math went out to meet Pryderi in battle.

But while he was away with his army, Gily, the lover, seized the beautiful maiden Goewen, who held the king's feet in her lap. She was not willing to marry Gily, but he eloped with her, and carried her off to his cottage.

The war which now raged was finally decided by single combat, as was the custom in old days. By this, the burning of the peasants' houses, and the ruin which threatened the whole country, ended, and peace came. It was not alone by the strength and fierceness of King Math, but also by the magic spells of Gwyd, that Pryderi was slain.

After burying the hero, King Math came back to his palace and found out what Gily had done. Then he took Goewen away from Gily, and to make amends for her trouble, in being thus torn from his palace, King Math made her his queen. Then the lovely Goewen shared his throne covered with the flame coloured satin. One of the most beautiful maidens of the court was chosen to hold his feet, until such time as a permanent choice was made.

As for the two nephews, who had fled from the wrath of their princely uncle, they were put under bans, as outlaws, and had to live on the borders of the kingdoms. No one of the king's people was allowed to give them food or drink. Yet they would not obey the summons of the king, to come and receive their punishment.

But at last, tired of being deserted by all good men and women, they repented in sorrow. Hungry, ragged and forlorn, they came to their uncle, the king to submit themselves to be punished. When they appeared, Math spoke roughly to them, and said, "You cannot make amends for the shame you have brought upon me. Yet, since you obey and are sorry, I shall punish you for a time and then pardon you. You are to do penance for three years at least."

Then they were changed into wild deer, and he told them to come back after twelve months. At the end of the year they returned, bringing with them a young fawn. As this creature was entirely innocent, it was given a human form and baptized in the church.

But the two brothers were changed into wild swine and driven off to find their food in the forest. At the end of the year, they came back with a young pig. The king had the little animal changed into a human being, which, like every mother's child in that time, received baptism.

Again, the brothers were transformed into animal shape. This time, as wolves, and were driven out to the hills. At the end of a twelve months' period, they came back, three in number, for one was a cub. By this time, the penance of the naughty nephews was over, and they were now to be delivered from all magic spells.

So their human nature was restored to them, but they must be washed thoroughly. In the first place, it took much hot water and lye, made from the wood ashes, and then a great deal of scrubbing, to make them presentable. Then they were anointed with sweet smelling oil, and the king ordered them to be arrayed in elegant apparel. They were appointed to hold honourable office at court, and from time to time to go out through the country, to call the officers to attend to public business.

When the time came that the king sought for one of the most beautiful maidens, who should hold his feet, Gwyd nominated to the prince's notice his sister Arianrod. The king was gracious, and thereafter she held his feet at all the banquets. She was looked up to with reverence by all and held the office for many years. Thus, King Math's reputation for grace and mercy was confirmed.

THE LONG-LIVED ANCESTORS

Adapted from Fairy-Tales & Other Stories by Peter Henry Emerson,
published by D. Nutt, London in 1894.

THE EAGLE OF GWERNABWY HAD BEEN long married to his female and had by her many chick-children. Sadly, one day she died, and the Eagle continued a long time a widower; but at length be proposed a marriage with the Owl of Cwm Cwmlwyd; but afraid of her being young, so as to have children by her, and thereby degrade his own family, he first of all went to inquire about her age amongst the aged of the world. Accordingly, he applied to the Stag of Rhedynfre, whom he found lying close to the trunk of an old oak and requested to know the Owl's age.

"I have seen," said the Stag, "this oak an acorn, which is now fallen to the ground through age, without either bark or leaves, and never suffered any hurt or strain except from my rubbing myself against it once a day, after getting up on my legs; but I never remember to have seen the Owl you mention younger or older than she seems to be at this day. But there is one older than I am, and that is the Salmon of Glynllifon."

The Eagle then applied to the Salmon for the age of the Owl. The Salmon answered, "I am as many years old as there are scales upon my skin, and particles of spawn within my belly; yet never saw I the Owl you mention but the same in appearance. But there is one older than I am, and that is the Blackbird of Cilgwri."

The Eagle next repaired to the Blackbird of Cilgwri, whom he found perched upon a small stone, and enquired of him the Owl's age.

"Dost you see this stone upon which I sit," said the Blackbird, "which is now no bigger than what a man can carry in his hand? I have seen this very stone of such weight as to be a sufficient load for a hundred oxen to draw, which has suffered neither rubbing nor wearing, save that I rub my bill on it once every evening, and touch the tips of my wings on it every morning, when I expand them to fly; yet I have not seen the Owl either older or younger than she appears to be at this day. But there is one older than I am, and that is the Frog of Mochno Bog, and if he does not know her age, there is not a creature living that does know it."

The Eagle went last of all to the Frog and desired to know the Owl's age. He answered, "I never ate anything but the dust from the spot which I inhabit, and that very sparingly, and dost you see these great hills that surround and overawe this bog where I lie? They are formed only of the excrements from my body since I have inhabited this place, yet I never remember to have seen the Owl but an old hag, making that hideous noise, Too, hoo, hoo! always frightening the children in the neighbourhood."

So, the Eagle of Gwernabwy, the Stag of Rhedynfre, the Salmon of Glynllifon, the Blackbird of Cilgwri, the Frog of Mochno Bog, and the Owl of Cwm Cwmlwyd are the oldest creatures in the whole world!

THE MAIDEN OF THE GREEN FOREST

Adapted from Welsh Fairy Tales by William Elliot Griffis and originally published in 1921.

MANY A PALACE LIES UNDER THE waves that wash Cymric land, for the sea has swallowed up more than one village, and even cities. When Welsh fairies yield to their mortal lovers and consent to become their wives, it is always on some condition or promise. Sometimes there are several of these, which the fairy ladies compel their mortal lovers to pledge them, before they agree to become wives. In fact, the fairies in Cymric land are among the most exacting of any known.

A prince named Benlli, of the Powys region, found this out to his grief, for he had always supposed that wives could be had simply for the asking. All that a man need say, to the girl to whom he took a fancy, was this, "Come along with me, and be my bride," and then she would say, "Thank you, I'll come," and the two would trot off together. This was the man's notion.

Now Benlli was a wicked old fellow. He was already married, but wrinkles had gathered on his wife's face. She had a faded, washed-out look, and her hair was thinning out. She would never be young again, and he was tired of her, and wanted a mate with fresh rosy cheeks, and long, thick hair. He was quite ready to fall in love with such a maiden, whenever his eyes should light upon her.

One day, he went out hunting in the Green Forest. While waiting for a wild boar to rush out, there rode past him a young woman whose beauty was dazzling. He instantly fell in love with her. The next day, while on horseback, at the same opening in the forest, the same maiden reappeared; but it was only for a moment, and then she vanished. Again, on the third day, the prince rode out to the appointed place, and again the vision of beauty was there. He rode up to her and begged her to come and live with him at his palace.

"I will come and be your wedded wife on three conditions: You must put away the wife you now have; you must permit me to leave you, one night in every seven, without following after or spying upon me; and you must not ask me where I go or what I do. Swear to me that you will do these three things. Then, if you keep your promises unbroken, my beauty shall never change, no, not until the tall vegetable flag-reeds wave and the long green rushes grow in your hall."

The Prince of Powys was quite ready to swear this oath and he solemnly promised to observe the three conditions. So, the Maid of the Green Forest went to live with him.

"But what of his old wife?" one asks. Ah! he had no trouble from that quarter, for when the newly-wedded couple arrived at the castle, she had already disappeared.

Happy, indeed, were the long bright days, which the prince and his new bride spent together, whether in the castle, or outdoors, riding on horseback, or in hunting the deer. Every day, her beauty seemed more divine, and she more lovely. He lavished various gifts upon her, among others that of a diadem of beryl and sapphire. Then he put on her finger a diamond ring worth what was a very great sum, a king's ransom. In the Middle Ages, monarchs as well as nobles were taken prisoners in battle and large amounts of money had to be paid to get them back again. So, a king's ransom is what Benlli paid for his wife's diamond ring. He loved her so dearly that he never suspected for a moment that he would ever have any trouble in keeping his three promises.

But without variety, life has no spice, and monotony wearies the soul. After nine years had passed, and his wife absented herself every Friday night, he began to wonder why it could be. His curiosity, to know the reason for her going away, so increased that it so wore on him that he became both miserable in himself and irritable toward others. Everybody in the castle noticed the change in their master and grieved over it.

One night, he invited a learned monk from the white monastery, not far away, to come and take dinner with him. The table in the great banqueting hall was spread with the most delicious viands, the lights were magnificent, and the music gay. But Wyland, the monk, was a man of magic and could see through things. He noticed that some secret grief was preying upon the Prince's mind. He discerned that, amidst all this splendour, he, Benlli, the lord of the castle, was the most miserable person within its walls. So Wyland went home, resolved to call again and find out what was the trouble.

When they met, some days later, Wyland's greeting was this, "Christ save thee, Benlli! What secret sorrow clouds your brow? Why so gloomy?"

Benlli at once burst out with the story of how he met the Maid of the Green Forest, and how she became his wife on three conditions.

"Think of it," said Benlli, groaning aloud. "When the owls cry and the crickets chirp, my wife leaves my bed, and until the daystar appears, I lie alone, torn with curiosity, to know where she is, and what she is doing. I fall again into heavy sleep, and do not awake until sunrise, when I find her by my side again. It is all such a mystery, that the secret lies heavy on my soul. Despite all my wealth, and my strong castle, with feasting and music by night and hunting by day, I am the most miserable man in Cymric land. No beggar is more wretched than I."

Wyland, the monk, listened and his eyes glittered. There came into his head the idea of enriching the monastery. He saw his chance and improved it at once. He could make money by solving the secret for a troubled soul. "Prince Benlli," said he, "if you will bestow upon the monks of the White Minster, one tenth of all the flocks that feed within your domain, and one tenth of all that flows into the vaults of your palace, and hand over the Maiden of the Green Forest to me, I shall warrant that your soul will be at peace and your troubles end."

To all this, Prince Benlli agreed, making solemn promise. Then the monk Wyland took his book, leather bound, and kept shut by means of metal clasps, and hid himself in the cranny of a rock near the Giant's Cave, from which there was entrance down into Fairyland. He had not long to wait, for soon, with a crown on her head, a lady, royally arrayed, passed by out of the silvery moonlight into the dark cave. It was none other than the Maiden of the Green Forest.

Now came a battle of magic and spells, as between the monk's own and those of the Green Forest Maiden. He moved forward to the mouth of the cave. Then summoning into his presence the spirits of the air and the cave, he informed them as to Benlli's vow to enrich the monastery, and to deliver the Green Forest Maiden to himself. Then, calling aloud, he said, "Let her forever be, as she now appears, and never leave my side. Bring her, before the break of day, to the cross near the town of the White Minster, and there will I wed her, and swear to make her my own."

Then, by the power of his magic, he made it impossible for any person or power to recall or hinder the operation of these words. Leaving the cave's mouth, in order to be at the cross, before day should dawn, the first thing he met was a hideous ogress, grinning and rolling her bleared red eyes at him. On her head seemed what was more like moss, than hair. She stretched out a long bony finger at him. On it, flashed the splendid diamond, which Benlli had given his bride, the beautiful Maid of the Green Forest.

"Take me to your bosom, monk Wyland," she shrieked, laughing hideously and showing what looked like green snags in her mouth. "For I am the wife you are sworn to wed. Thirty years ago, I was Benlli's blooming bride. When my beauty left me, his love flew out of the window. Now I am a foul ogress, but magic makes me young again every seventh night. I promised that my beauty should last until the tall flag reeds and the long green rushes grow in his hall."

Amazed at her story, Wyland drew in his breath.

"And this promise, I have kept. It is already fulfilled. Your spell and mine are both completed. Yours brought to him the peace of the dead. Mine made the river floods rush in. Now, waters lap to and fro among the reeds and rushes that grow in the banqueting hall, which is now sunk deep below the earth. With the clash of our spells, no charm can redress our fate.

"Come then and take me as your bride, for oath and spell have both decreed it as your reward. As Benlli's promise to you is fulfilled, for the waters flow in the palace vaults, the pike and the dare feed there."

So, caught in his own dark, sordid plot, the monk, who played conjurer, had become the victim of his own craft. They say that Wyland's Cross still recalls the monk, while fishermen on the Welsh border, can, on nights with smooth water, see towers and chimneys far below, sunk deep beneath the waves.

THE MIGHTY MONSTER AFANG

Adapted from Welsh Fairy Tales by William Elliot Griffis and originally published in 1921.

AFTER THE CYMRIC FOLK, THAT IS, the people we call Welsh, had come up from Cornwall into their new land, they began to cut down the trees, to build towns, and to have fields and gardens. Soon they made the landscape smile with pleasant homes, rich farms and playing children. They trained vines and made flowers grow. The young folks made pets of the wild animals' cubs, which their fathers and big brothers brought home from hunting. Old men took rushes and reeds and wove them into cages for songbirds to live in.

While they were draining the swamps and bogs, they drove out the monsters, that had made their lair in these wet places. These terrible creatures liked to poison people with their bad breath, and even ate up very little boys and girls, when they strayed away from home.

So, all the face of the open country between the forests became very pretty to look at. The whole of Cymric land, which then extended from the northern Grampian Hills to Cornwall, and from the Irish Sea, past their big fort, afterward called London, even to the edge of the German Ocean, became a delightful place to live in.

The lowlands and the rivers, in which the tide rose and fell daily, were especially attractive. This was chiefly because of the many bright flowers growing there; while the yellow gorse and the pink heather made the hills look as lovely as a young girl's face. Besides this, the Cymric maidens were the prettiest ever, and the lads were all brave and healthy; while both of these knew how to sing often and well.

While all this went on there was still one great monster named the Afang, that lived in a big bog, hidden among the high hills and inside of a dark, rough forest. This ugly creature had an iron-clad back and a long tail that could wrap itself around a mountain. It had four front legs, with big knees that were bent up like a grasshopper's but were covered with scales like armour. These were as hard as steel and bulged out at the thighs. Along its back, was a ridge of horns, like spines, and higher than an alligator's. Against such a tough hide, when the hunters shot their darts and hurled their javelins, these weapons fell down to the ground, like harmless pins.

On this monster's head, were big ears, halfway between those of a jackass and an elephant. Its eyes were as green as leeks, and were round, but scalloped on the edges, like squashes, while they were as big as pumpkins.

The Afang's face was much like a monkey's, or a gorilla's, with long straggling grey hairs around its cheeks like those of a walrus. It always looked as if a napkin, as big as a bath towel, would be necessary to keep its mouth clean. Yet even then, it slobbered a good deal, so that no nice fairy liked to be near the monster. When the Afang growled, the bushes shook, and the oak leaves trembled on the branches, as if a strong wind was blowing.

But after its dinner, when it had swallowed down a man, or two calves, or four sheep, or a fat heifer, or three goats, its body swelled up like a balloon. Then it usually rolled over, lay along the ground, or in the soft mud, and felt very stupid and sleepy, for a long while. All around its lair, lay wagon loads of bones of the creatures, girls, women, men, boys, cows, and occasionally a donkey, which it had devoured.

But when the Afang was ravenously hungry and could not get these animals and when fat girls and careless boys were scarce, it would live on birds, beasts and fishes. Although it was very fond of cows and sheep, yet the wool and hair of these animals stuck in its big teeth, it often felt very miserable and the creature's usually bad temper grew worse. Then, like a beaver, it would cut down a tree, sharpen it to a point and pick its teeth until its mouth was clean. Yet it seemed all the more hungry and eager for fresh human victims to eat, especially juicy maidens; just as children like cake more than bread.

The Cymric men were not surprised at this, for they knew that girls were very sweet and they almost worshiped women. So, they learned to guard their daughters and wives. They saw that to do such things as eating up people was in the nature of the beast, which could never be taught good manners.

But what made them mad beyond measure was the trick which the monster often played upon them by breaking the river banks, and the dykes which with great toil they had built to protect their crops. Then the waters overflowed all their farms, ruined their gardens and spoiled their cow houses and stables.

This sort of mischief the Afang liked to play, especially about the time when the oat and barley crops were ripe and ready to be gathered to make cakes and flummery; that is sour oat-jelly, or pap. So, it often happened that the children had to do without their cookies and porridge during the winter. Sometimes the floods rose so high as to wash away the houses and float the cradles. Even those with little babies in them were often seen on the raging waters, and sent dancing on the waves down the river, to the sea. Once in a while, a mother cat and all her kittens were seen meowing for help, or a lady dog howling piteously. Often it happened that both puppies and kittens were drowned.

So, whether for men or mothers, pussies or puppies, the Cymric men thought the time had come to stop this monster's mischief. It was bad enough that people should be eaten up, but to have all their crops ruined and animals drowned, so that they had to go hungry all winter, with only a little fried fish, and no turnips, was too much for human patience. There were too many weeping mothers and sorrowful fathers, and squalling brats and animals whining for something to eat.

Besides, if all the oats were washed away, how could their wives make flummery, without which, no Cymric man is ever happy? And where would they get seed for another year's sowing? And if there were no cows, how could the babies or kitties live, or any grown-up persons get buttermilk?

Someone may ask, why did not some brave man shoot the Afang, with a poisoned arrow, or drive a spear into him under the arms, where the flesh was tender, or cut off his head with a sharp sword? The trouble was just here. There were plenty of brave fellows, ready to fight the monster, but nothing made of iron could pierce that hide of his. This was like armour, or one of the steel battleships of our day, and the Afang always spit out fire or poison breath down the road, up which a man was coming, long before the brave fellow could get near him. Nothing would do, but to go up into his lair, and drag him out.

But what man or company of men was strong enough to do this, when a dozen giants in a gang, with ropes as thick as a ship's hawser, could hardly tackle the job? Nevertheless, in what neither man nor giant could do, a pretty maiden might succeed. True, she must be brave also, for how could she know, but if hungry, the Afang might eat her up?

However, one valiant damsel, of great beauty, who had lots of perfumery and plenty of pretty clothes, volunteered to bind the monster in his lair. She said, "I'm not afraid." Her sweetheart was named Gadern, and he was a young and strong hunter. He talked over the matter with her and they two resolved to act together.

Gadern went all over the country, summoning the farmers to bring their ox teams and log chains. Then he set the blacksmiths to work, forging new and especially heavy ones, made of the best native iron, from the mines, for which Wales is still famous.

Meanwhile, the lovely maiden arrayed herself in her prettiest clothes, dressed her hair in the most enticing way, hanging a white blossom on each side, over her ears, with one flower also at her neck. When she had perfumed her garments, she sallied forth and up the lake where the big bog and the waters were and where the monster hid himself.

While the maiden was still quite a distance away, the terrible Afang, scenting his visitor from afar, came rushing out of his lair. When very near, he reared his head high in the air, expecting to pounce on her, with his ironclad claws and at one swallow make a breakfast of the girl.

But the odours of her perfumes were so sweet, that he forgot what he had thought to do. Moreover, when he looked at her, he was so taken with unusual beauty, that he flopped at once on his forefeet. Then he behaved just like a lovelorn beau, when his best girl comes near. He ties his necktie and pulls down his coat and brushes off the collar, and so the Afang began to spruce up. It was real fun to see how a monster behaves when smitten with love for a pretty girl. He had no idea how funny he was.

The girl was not at all afraid, but smoothed the monster's back, stroked and played with its big moustaches and tickled its neck until the Afang's throat actually gurgled with a laugh. Pretty soon he guffawed, for he was so delighted. When he did this, the people down in the valley thought it was thunder, though the sky was clear and blue.

The maiden tickled his chin, and even put up his whiskers in curl papers. Then she stroked his neck, so that his eyes closed. Soon she had gently lulled him to slumber, by singing a cradle song, which her mother had taught her. This she did so softly, and sweetly, that in a few minutes, with its head in her lap, the monster was sound asleep and even began to snore.

Then, quietly, from their hiding places in the bushes, Gadern and his men crawled out. When near the dreaded Afang, they stood up and sneaked forward, very softly on tip toe. They had wrapped the links of the chain in grass and leaves, so that no clanking was heard. They also held the oxen's yokes, so that nobody or anything could rattle, or make any noise. Slowly but surely, they passed the chain over its body, in the middle, besides binding the brute securely between its fore and hind legs. And all this time, the monster slept on, for the girl kept on crooning her melody.

When the forty yoke of oxen were all harnessed together, the drovers cracked all their whips at once, so that it sounded like a clap of thunder and the whole team began to pull together. Then the Afang woke up with a start. The sudden jerk roused the monster to wrath, and its bellowing was terrible. It rolled round and round, and dug its four sets of toes, each with three claws, each and every one as big as a ploughshare, into the ground. It tried hard to crawl into its lair or slip into the lake.

Finding that neither was possible, the Afang looked about, for some big tree to wrap its tail around. But all his writhings or plungings were of no use. The drovers plied their whips and the oxen kept on with one long pull together and forward. They strained so hard, that one of them dropped its eye out. This formed a pool, and to this day they call it The Pool of the Ox's Eye. It never dries up or overflows, though the water in it rises and falls, as regularly as the tides.

For miles over the mountains the sturdy oxen hauled the monster. The pass over which they toiled and strained so hard is still named the Pass of the Oxen's Slope. When going downhill, the work of dragging the Afang was easier.

In a great hole in the ground, big enough to be a pond, they dumped the carcass of the Afang, and soon a little lake was formed. This uncanny bit of water is called "The Lake of the Green Well." It is considered dangerous for man or beast to go too near it. Birds do not like to fly over the surface, and when sheep tumble in, they sink to the bottom at once.

If the bones of the Afang still lie at the bottom, they must have sunk down very deep, for the monster had no more power to get out, or to break the river banks. The farmers no longer cared anything about the creature, and they hardly every think of the old story, except when a sheep is lost.

As for Gadern and his brave and lovely sweetheart, they were married and lived long and happily. Their descendants, in the thirty-seventh generation, are proud of the grand exploit of their ancestors, while all the farmers honour his memory and bless the name of the lovely girl that put the monster asleep.

THE OLD MAN AND THE FAIRIES

Adapted from Fairy-Tales & Other Stories by Peter Henry Emerson,
published by D. Nutt, London in 1894.

MANY YEARS AGO, THE WELSH MOUNTAINS were full of fairies. People used to go by moonlight to see them dancing, for they knew where they would dance by seeing green rings in the grass.

There was an old man living in those days who used to frequent the fairs that were held across the mountains. One day he was crossing the mountains to a fair, and when he got to a lonely valley he sat down, for he was tired, and he dropped off to sleep, and his bag fell down by his side. When he was sound asleep the fairies came and carried him off, bag and all, and took him under the earth, and when he awoke he found himself in a great palace of gold, full of fairies dancing and singing. And they took him and showed him everything, the splendid gold room and gardens, and they kept dancing round him until he fell asleep.

When he was asleep they carried him back to the same spot where they had found him, and when he awoke he thought he had been dreaming, so he looked for his bag, and got hold of it, but he could hardly lift it. When he opened it he found it was nearly filled with gold.

He managed to pick it up, and turning around, he went home.

When he got home, his wife Kaddy said, "What's to do, why haven't you been to the fair?"

"I've got something here," he said, and showed his wife the gold.

"Why, where did you get that?"

But he wouldn't tell her. Since she was curious, like all women, she kept worrying him all night, for he'd put the money in a box under the bed, and so he told her about the fairies.

Next morning, when he awoke, he thought he'd go to the fair and buy a lot of things, and he went to the box to get some of the gold but found it full of cockle-shells.

THE PENTREFOELAS LEGEND

*Adapted from Welsh Folk-Lore by Owain Elias, published in 1896
by Woodall, Minshall and Co, and based on Elias' prize essay of
the national Eisteddfod, 1887.*

THE SON OF HAFOD GARREG WAS shepherding his father's flock on the hills, and whilst thus engaged, he, one misty morning, came suddenly upon a lovely girl, seated on the sheltered side of a peat-stack. The maiden appeared to be in great distress, and she was crying bitterly. The young man went up to her, and spoke kindly to her, and his attention and sympathy were not without effect on the comely stranger.

So beautiful was the young woman, that from expressions of sympathy the smitten youth proceeded to words of love, and his advances were not repelled. But whilst the lovers were holding sweet conversation, there appeared on the scene a venerable and aged man, who, addressing the female as her father, bade her follow him. She immediately obeyed, and both departed leaving the young man alone.

He lingered about the place until the evening, wishing and hoping that she might return, but she came not. Early the next day, he was at the spot where he first felt what love was. All day long he loitered about the place, vainly hoping that the beautiful girl would pay another visit to the mountain, but he was doomed to disappointment, and night again drove him homewards. Thus, daily went he to the place where he had met his beloved, but she was not there, and, love-sick and lonely, he returned to Hafod Garreg.

Such devotion deserved its reward. It would seem that the young lady loved the young man quite as much as he loved her. And in yn nhir hud a lledrith (the land of allurement and illusion) she planned a visit to the earth to meet her lover, but she was soon missed by her father, and he, suspecting her love for this young man, again came upon them, and found them conversing lovingly together.

Much talk took place between the sire and his daughter, and the shepherd, waxing bold, begged and begged her father to give him his daughter in marriage. The sire, perceiving that the man was in earnest, turned to his daughter, and asked her whether it was her wish to marry a man of the earth? She said it was. Then the father told the shepherd he should have his daughter to wife, and that she should stay with him, until he should strike her with iron, and that, as a marriage portion, he would give her a bag filled with bright money.

The young couple were duly married, and the promised dowry was received. For many years they lived lovingly and happily together, and children were born to them. One day this man and his wife went together to the hill to catch a couple of ponies, to carry them to the Festival of the Saint of Capel Garmon. The ponies were very wild and could not be caught. The man, irritated, pursued the nimble creatures. His wife was by his side, and now he thought he had them in his power, but just at the moment he was about to grasp their manes, off they wildly galloped, and the man, in anger, finding that they had again eluded him, threw the bridle after them, and, sad to say, the bit struck the wife, and as this was of iron they both knew that their marriage contract was broken.

Hardly had they had time to realise the dire accident, ere the aged father of the bride appeared, accompanied by a host of Fairies, and there and then departed with his daughter to the land whence she came, and that, too, without even allowing her to bid farewell to her children. The money, though, and the children were left behind, and these were the only memorials of the lovely wife and the kindest of mothers, that remained to remind the shepherd of the treasure he had lost in the person of his Fairy spouse.

THE RED BANDITS OF MONTGOMERY

Adapted from Welsh Fairy Tales by William Elliot Griffis and originally published in 1921.

WHEN CHIMNEYS WERE FIRST ADDED TO houses in Wales, and the style of house-building changed, from round to square, many old people found fault with the new fashion of letting the smoke out. They declared they caught colds and sneezed oftener than in the times gone by. The chimneys, they said, cost too much money, and were useless extravagances. They got along well enough, in the good old days, when the smoke had its own way of getting out. Then, it took plenty of time to pass through the doors and wind holes, for no one person or thing was in a hurry, when they were young. Moreover, when the fireplace was in the middle of the floor, the whole family sat around it and had a sociable time.

It was true, as they confessed, when argued with, that the smell of the cooking used to linger too long. The soot also, hung in long streamers from the rafters, and stuck to the house, like old friends. But the greatest and most practical objection of the old folks to the chimneys was that robbers used them to climb down at night and steal people's money, when they were asleep. So, many householders used to set old scythe blades across the new smoke holes, to keep out the thieves, or to slice them up, if they persisted. In Montgomery, which is one of the Welsh shires, there was an epidemic of robbery, and the doings of the Red Bandits are famous in history.

Now there was a young widow, whose husband had been killed by the footpads, or road robbers. She was left alone in the world, with a little boy baby in the cradle and only one cow in the byre. She had hard work to pay her rent, but as there were three or four scythes set in the chimney, and the cow stable had a good lock on it, she thought she was safe from burglars or common thieves.

But the Red Bandits picked out the most expert chimney-climber in their gang, and he one night slipped down into the widow's cottage, without making any noise or cutting off his nose, toes, or fingers. Then, robbing the widow of her rent money, he picked the lock of the byre and drove off the cow. In the morning, the poor woman found both doors open, but there was no money and no cow.

While she was crying over her loss, and wringing her hands, because of her poverty, she heard a knock at the door. "Come in," said the widow.

There entered an old lady with a kindly face. She was very tall and well dressed. Her cloak, her gloves, and shoes, and the ruffles under her high peaked Welsh headdress, were all green. The widow thought she looked like an animated leek. In her right hand was a long staff, and in her left, under her cloak, she held a little bag, that was green, also.

"Why do you weep?" asked the visitor.

Then the widow told her tale of woe; the story of the loss of her husband, and how a red robber, in spite of the scythe blades set in the chimney, had come down and taken away both her money and her cow. Now, although she had sold all her butter and cream, she could neither pay her rent, nor have any buttermilk with her rye bread and flummery.

"Dry your tears and take comfort," said the tall lady in the green peaked hat. "Here is money enough to pay your rent and buy another cow." With that, she sat down at the round table near the peat fire. Opening her bag, the shining gold coins slid out and formed a little heap on the table. "There, you can have all this, if you will give me all I want."

At first, the widow's eyes opened wide, and then she glanced at the cradle, where her baby was sleeping. Then she wondered, though she said nothing. But the next moment, she was laughing at herself, and looking around at her poor cottage. She tried to guess what there was in it, that the old lady could possibly want. "You can have anything I have. Name it," she said cheerfully to her visitor. But only a moment more, and all her fears returned at the thought that the visitor might ask for her boy.

The old lady spoke again and said, "I want to help you all I can, but what I came here for is to get the little boy in the cradle."

The widow now saw that the old woman was a fairy, and that if her visitor got hold of her son, she would never see her child again. So she begged piteously of the old lady, to take anything and everything, except her one child.

"No, I want that boy, and, if you want the gold, you must let me take him."

"Is there anything else that I can do for you, so that I may get the money?" asked the widow.

"Well, I'll make it easier for you. There are two things I must tell you to cheer you."

"What are they?" asked the widow, eagerly.

"One is, that by our fairy law, I cannot take your boy, until three days have passed. Then, I shall come again, and you shall have the gold; but only on the one condition I have stated."

"And the next?" almost gasped the widow.

"If you can guess my name, you will doubly win; for then, I shall give you the gold and you can keep your boy." Without waiting for another word, the lady in green scooped up her money, put it back in the bag, and moved off and out the door.

The poor woman, at once a widow and mother, and now stripped of her property, fearing to lose her boy, brooded all night over her troubles and never slept a wink. In the morning, she rose up, left her baby with a neighbour, and went to visit some relatives in the next village, which was several miles distant. She told her story, but her kinsfolk were too poor to help her. So, all disconsolate, she turned her face homewards.

On her way back she had to pass through the woods, where, on one side, was a clearing. In the middle of this open space, was a ring of grass. In the ring a little fairy lady was tripping around and singing to herself.

Creeping up silently, the anxious mother heard to her joy, a rhymed couplet and caught the sound of a name, several times repeated. It sounded like "Silly Doot."

Hurrying home and perfectly sure that she knew the secret that would save her boy, she set cheerily about her regular work and daily tasks. In fact, she slept soundly that night. Next day, in came the lady in green as before, with her bag of money. Taking her seat at the round table, near the fire, she poured out the gold. Then jingling the coins in the pile, she said:

"Now give up your boy, or guess my name, if you want me to help you."

The young widow, feeling sure that she had the old fairy in a trap, thought she would have some fun first. "How many guesses am I allowed?" she asked.

"All you want, and as many as you please," answered the green lady, smiling.

The widow rattled off a string of names, English, Welsh and Biblical; but every time the fairy shook her head. Her eyes began to gleam, as if she felt certain of getting the boy. She even moved her chair around to the side nearest the cradle.

"One more guess," cried the widow. "Can it be Silly Doot?"

At this sound, the fairy turned red with rage. At the same moment, the door opened wide and a blast of wind made the hearth fire flare up. Leaving her gold behind her, the old woman flew up the chimney, and disappeared over the housetops.

The widow scooped up the gold, bought two cows, furnished her cottage with new chairs and fresh flowers, and put the rest of the coins away under one of the flag stones at the hearth. When her boy grew up, she gave him a good education, and he became one of the fearless judges, who, with the aid of Baron Owen, rooted out of their lair the Red Bandits, that had robbed his mother. Since that day, there has been little crime in Wales - the best governed part of the kingdom.

THE SHEPHERD OF MYDDVAI

Adapted from Welsh Folk-Lore by Owain Elias, published in 1896 by Woodall, Minshall and Co, and based on Elias' prize essay of the national Eisteddfod, 1887.

A WIDOW, WHO HAD AN ONLY son, was obliged, in consequence of the large flocks that she possessed, to send her sheep to distant pastures. Up in the Black Mountains in Carmarthenshire lies the lake known as Lyn y Van Vach. To the shores of this lake the shepherd of Myddvai would lead his lambs and lay there whilst they sought pasture.

Suddenly, from the dark waters of the lake, he saw three maidens rise. Shaking the bright drops from their hair and gliding to the shore, they wandered about amongst his flock. They had more than mortal beauty, and he was filled with love for her that came nearest to him. He offered her the bread he had with him, and she took it and tried it, but then sang to him:

Hard-baked is your bread,

'Tis not easy to catch me.

She then ran off laughing towards the lake.

On his return home he communicated to his mother the extraordinary vision. She advised him to take some unbaked dough the next time in his pocket, as there must have been some spell connected with the hard-baked bread, or "Bara Cras," which prevented his catching the lady

Next morning, before the sun was up, the young man was at the lake, not for the purpose of looking after the cattle, but that he might again witness the enchanting vision of the previous day. In vain did he glance over the surface of the lake; nothing met his view, save the ripples occasioned by a stiff breeze, and a dark cloud hung heavily on the summit of the Van.

Hours passed on, the wind was hushed, the overhanging clouds had vanished, when the youth was startled by seeing some of his mother's cattle on the precipitous side of the acclivity, nearly on the opposite side of the lake. As he was hastening away to rescue them from their perilous position, the object of his search again appeared to him, and seemed much more beautiful than when he first beheld her. His hand was again held out to her, full of unbaked bread, which he offered to her with an urgent proffer of his heart also, and vows of eternal attachment, all of which were refused by her, saying

Unbaked is your bread,

I will not have thee.

Once again, she disappeared in the waves. But the smiles that played upon her features as the lady vanished beneath the waters forbade him to despair and cheered him on his way home. His aged parent was acquainted with his ill success, and she suggested that his bread should the next time be but slightly baked, as most likely to please the mysterious being.

Impelled by love, the youth left his mother's home early next morning. He was soon near the margin of the lake impatiently awaiting the reappearance of the lady. The sheep and goats browsed on the precipitous sides of the Van, the cattle strayed amongst the rocks, rain and sunshine came and passed away, unheeded by the youth who was wrapped up in looking for the appearance of her who had stolen his heart.

The sun was verging towards the west, and the young man casting a sad look over the waters ere departing homewards was astonished to see several cows walking along its surface, and, what was more pleasing to his sight, the maiden reappeared, even lovelier than ever. She approached the land and he rushed to meet her in the water. A smile encouraged him to seize her hand, and she accepted the moderately baked bread he offered her.

Thus, the Lady of the Lake became engaged to the young man, and having taken her hand for a moment she darted away and dived into the lake. The grief of the lover at this disappearance of his affianced was such that he determined to cast himself headlong into its unfathomed depths, and thus end his life. As he was on the point of committing this rash act, there emerged out of the lake two most beautiful ladies, accompanied by a hoary-headed man of noble mien and extraordinary stature, but having otherwise all the force and strength of youth. This man addressed the youth, saying that, as he proposed to marry one of his daughters, he consented to the union, provided the young man could distinguish which of the two ladies before him was the object of his affections. This was no easy task, as the maidens were perfect counterparts of each other.

Whilst the young man narrowly scanned the two ladies and failed to perceive the least difference betwixt the two, one of them thrust her foot a slight degree forward. The motion, simple as it was, did not escape the observation of the youth, and he discovered a trifling variation in the mode in which their sandals were tied. This at once put an end to the dilemma, for he had on previous occasions noticed the peculiarity of her shoe-tie, and he boldly took hold of her hand.

"You have chosen rightly," said the Father, "be to her a kind and faithful husband, and I will give her, as a dowry, as many sheep, cattle, goats, and horses, as she can count of each without heaving or drawing in her breath. But remember, that if you prove unkind to her at any time and strike her three times without a cause, she shall return to me, and shall bring all her stock with her."

Such was the marriage settlement, to which the young man gladly assented, and the bride was desired to count the number of sheep she was to have. She immediately adopted the mode of counting by fives; one, two, three, four, five, - one, two, three, four, five; as many times as possible in rapid succession, till her breath was exhausted. The same process of reckoning had to determine the number of goats, cattle, and horses, respectively; and in an instant the full number of each came out of the lake, when called upon by the Father.

The young couple were then married, and went to reside at a farm called Esgair Llaethdy, near Myddvai, where they lived in prosperity and happiness for several years and became the parents of three beautiful sons.

Once upon a time there was a christening in the neighbourhood to which the parents were invited. When the day arrived, the wife appeared reluctant to attend the christening, alleging that the distance was too great for her to walk. Her husband told her to fetch one of the horses from the field. "I will," said she, "if you will bring me my gloves which I left in our house." He went for the gloves, and finding she had not gone for the horse, he playfully slapped her shoulder with one of them, saying "dôs, dôs, go, go," when she reminded him of the terms on which she consented to marry him, and warned him to be more cautious in the future, as he had now given her one causeless blow.

On another occasion when they were together at a wedding and the assembled guests were greatly enjoying themselves the wife burst into tears and sobbed most piteously. Her husband touched her on the shoulder and inquired the cause of her weeping; she said, "Now people are entering into trouble, and your troubles are likely to commence, as you have the second time stricken me without a cause."

Years passed on, and their children had grown up, and were particularly clever young men. Amidst so many worldly blessings the husband almost forgot that only one causeless blow would destroy his prosperity. Still he was watchful lest any trivial occurrence should take place which his wife must regard as a breach of their marriage contract. She told him that her affection for him was unabated and warned him to be careful lest through inadvertence he might give the last and only blow which, by an unalterable destiny, over which she had no control, would separate them forever.

One day it happened that they went to a funeral together, where, in the midst of mourning and grief at the house of the deceased, she appeared in the gayest of spirits, and indulged in inconsiderate fits of laughter, which so shocked her husband that he touched her, saying, "Hush! hush! don't laugh." She said that she laughed because people when they die go out of trouble, and rising up, she went out of the house, saying, "The last blow has been struck, our marriage contract is broken, and at an end. Farewell!" Then she started off towards Esgair Llaethdy, where she called her cattle and other stock together, each by name, not forgetting, the "little black calf" which had been slaughtered and was suspended on the hook, and away went the calf and all the stock, with the Lady across Myddvai Mountain, and disappeared beneath the waters of the lake whence the Lady had come. The four oxen that were ploughing departed, drawing after them the plough, which made a furrow in the ground, and which remains as a testimony of the truth of this story.

She is said to have appeared to her sons, and accosting Rhiwallon, her firstborn, to have informed him that he was to be a benefactor to mankind, through healing all manner of their diseases, and she furnished him with prescriptions and instructions for the preservation of health. Then, promising to meet him when her counsel was most needed, she vanished. On several other occasions she met her sons, and pointed out to them plants and herbs, and revealed to them their medicinal qualities or virtues.

So ends the Myddvai Legend.

THE SILVER SHILLINGS

Adapted from Welsh Folk-Lore by Owain Elias, published in 1896 by Woodall, Minshall and Co, and based on Elias' prize essay of the national Eisteddfod, 1887.

THE FOLLOWING TALE WAS TOLD TO Owain Elias by Thomas Jones, a small mountain farmer, who occupied land near Pont Petrual, a place between Ruthin and Llanfihangel Glyn Myfyr. Jones informed Elias that he was acquainted with all the parties mentioned in the tale. His story was as follows:

A shoemaker, whose health would not permit him to pursue his own trade, obtained work in a tan yard at Penybont, near Corwen. The shoemaker lived in a house called Ty'n-y-graig, belonging to Clegir isa farm.

He walked daily to his employment, a distance of several miles, because he could not afford to pay for lodgings. One day, he noticed a round bit of green ground, close to one of the gates on Tan-y-Coed farm and going up to it discovered a piece of silver lying on the sward.

Day after day, from the same spot, he picked up a silver coin. By this means, as well as by the wage he received, he became a well-to-do man. His wife noticed the many new coins he brought home, and questioned him about them, but he kept the secret of their origin to himself. At last, however, in consequence of repeated inquiries, he told her all about the silver pieces, which daily he had picked up from the green plot.

The next day he passed the place, but there was no silver, as in days gone by, and he never discovered another shilling, although he looked for it every day. The poor man did not live long after he had informed his wife whence he had obtained the bright silver coins.

THE SON OF LLECH Y DERWYDD

Adapted from Welsh Folk-Lore by Owain Elias, published in 1896 by Woodall, Minshall and Co, and based on Elias' prize essay of the national Eisteddfod, 1887.

THE SON OF LLECH Y DERWYDD was the only son of his parents and heir to the farm. He was very dear to his father and mother, yea, he was as the very light of their eyes. The son and the head servant man were bosom friends, they were like two brothers, or rather twins. As they were such close friends the farmer's wife was in the habit of clothing them exactly alike.

The two friends fell in love with two young handsome women who were highly respected in the neighbourhood. This event gave the old people great satisfaction, and ere long the two couples were joined in holy wedlock, and great was the merry-making on the occasion. The servant man obtained a convenient place to live in on the grounds of Llech y Derwydd.

About six months after the marriage of the son, he and the servant man went out to hunt. The servant penetrated to a ravine filled with brushwood to look for game, and presently returned to his friend, but by the time he came back the son was nowhere to be seen. He continued awhile looking about for his absent friend, shouting and whistling to attract his attention, but there was no answer to his calls.

By and by the servant man went home to Llech y Derwydd, expecting to find his friend there, but no one knew anything about him. Great was the grief of the family throughout the night, but it was even greater the next day. They went to inspect the place where the son had last been seen. His mother and his wife wept bitterly, but the father had greater control over himself, but even he still appeared as half mad.

They inspected the place where the servant man had last seen his friend, and, to their great surprise and sorrow, observed a Fairy ring close by the spot, and the servant recollected that he had heard seductive music somewhere about the time that he parted with his friend. They came to the conclusion at once that the man had been so unfortunate as to enter the Fairy ring, and they conjectured that he had been transported no one knew where.

Weary weeks and months passed away, and a son was born to the absent man. The little one grew up the very image of his father, and very precious was he to his grandfather and grandmother. In fact, he was everything to them. He grew up to man's estate and married a pretty girl in the neighbourhood, but her people had not the reputation of being kind-hearted. The old folks died, and also their daughter-in-law.

One windy afternoon in the month of October, the family of Llech y Derwydd saw a tall thin old man with beard and hair as white as snow, who they thought was a Peddler, approaching slowly, very slowly, towards the house. The servant girls stared mockingly through the window at him, and their mistress laughed unfeelingly at the "old Wretch," and lifted the children up, one after the other, to get a sight of him as he neared the house.

He came to the door, and entered the house boldly enough, and inquired after his parents. The mistress answered him in a surly and unusually contemptuous manner and wished to know "What the drunken old peddler wanted there," for they thought he must have been drinking or he would never have spoken in the way he did.

The old man looked at everything in the house with surprise and bewilderment, but the little children about the floor took his attention more than anything else. His looks betrayed sorrow and deep disappointment. He related his whole history, that, yesterday he had gone out to hunt, and that he had now returned. The mistress told him that she had heard a story about her husband's father, which occurred before she was born, that he had been lost whilst hunting, but that her father had told her that the story was not true, but that he had been killed.

The woman became uneasy and angry that the old man did not depart. The old man was roused and said that the house was his, and that he would have his rights. He went to inspect his possessions, and shortly afterwards directed his steps to the servant's house. To his surprise he saw that things there were greatly changed.

After conversing awhile with an aged man who sat by the fire, they carefully looked each other in the face, and the old man by the fire related the sad history of his lost friend, the son of Llech y Derwydd. They conversed together deliberately on the events of their youth, but all seemed like a dream. However, the old man in the corner came to the conclusion that his visitor was his dear friend, the son of Llech y Derwydd, returned from the land of the Fairies after having spent there half a hundred years.

The old man with the white beard believed the story related by his friend, and long was the talk and many were the questions which the one gave to the other. The visitor was informed that the master of Llech y Derwydd was from home that day, and he was persuaded to eat some food; but, to the horror of all, when he had done so, he instantly fell down dead.

THE SPELLBOUND MAN

Adapted from Welsh Folk-Lore by Owain Elias, published in 1896 by Woodall, Minshall and Co, and based on Elias' prize essay of the national Eisteddfod, 1887.

A PENTREFOELAS MAN WAS COMING HOME one lovely summer's night when, within a stone's throw of his house, he heard in the far distance singing of the most enchanting kind.

He stopped to listen to the sweet sounds which filled him with a sensation of deep pleasure. He had not listened long ere he perceived that the singers were approaching. By and by they came to the spot where he was, and he saw that they were marching in single file and consisted of a number of small people, robed in close-fitting grey clothes, and they were accompanied by speckled dogs that marched along two deep like soldiers.

When the procession came quite opposite the enraptured listener, it stopped, and the small people spoke to him and earnestly begged him to accompany them, but he would not. They tried many ways, and for a long time, to persuade him to join them, but when they saw they could not induce him to do so they departed, dividing themselves into two companies and marching away, the dogs marching two abreast in front of each company. They sang as they went away the most entrancing music that was ever heard.

The man stood where he was, utterly spellbound, listening to the ravishing music of the Fairies, and he did not enter his house until the last sound had died away in the far-off distance.

THE STORY OF THE PIG-TROUGH

Adapted from Fairy-Tales & Other Stories by Peter Henry Emerson,
published by D. Nutt, London in 1894.

AT THE BEGINNING OF THE NINETEENTH century, Dafydd Hughes went as military substitute in place of a rich farmer's son. He got £80, a watch, and a suit of clothes.

His mother was loath to let him go, and when he joined his regiment, she followed him from Amlwch to Pwllheli to try and buy him off. He would not hear of it.

"Mother," he said, "the whole of Anglesey would not keep me, I want to be off, and see the world."

The regiment was quartered in Edinboro', and Hughes married the daughter of the burgess with whom he was billeted.

Thence, leaving a small son, as hostage to the grandparents, they went to Ireland, and Hughes and his wife were billeted on a pork-butcher's family in Dublin.

One day, the mother of the pork-butcher, an old granny, told them she had seen the fairies.

"Last night, as I was abed, I saw a bright, bright light come in, and afterwards a troop of little angels. They danced all over my bed, and they played and sang music - oh! the sweetest music ever I heard. I lay and watched them and listened. Bye-and-bye the light went out and the music stopped, and I saw them no more. I regretted the music very much.

"But directly after another smaller light appeared, and a tall dark man came up to my bed, and with something in his hand he tapped me on the temple; it felt like someone drawing a sharp pin across my temple then he went too. In the morning my pillow was covered with blood.

"I thought and thought, and then I knew I had moved the pig's trough and must have put it in the fairies' path and the fairies were angered, and the king of the fairies had punished me for it."

She moved the trough back to its old place the next day and received no more visits from the wee folk.

THE TALE OF IVAN

Adapted from Celtic Fairy Tales by Joseph Jacobs, originally published in 1891.

THERE WERE FORMERLY A MAN AND a woman living in the parish of Llanlavan, in the place which is called Hwrdh. And work became scarce, so the man said to his wife, "I will go search for work, and you may live here." So, he took fair leave, and travelled far toward the East, and at last came to the house of a farmer and asked for work.

"What work can ye do?" said the farmer.

"I can do all kinds of work," said Ivan.

Then they agreed upon three pounds for the year's wages.

When the end of the year came his master showed him the three pounds. "See, Ivan," said he, "here's your wage; but if you will give it me back I'll give you a piece of advice instead."

"Give me my wage," said Ivan.

"No, I'll not," said the master; "I'll explain my advice."

"Tell it me, then," said Ivan.

Then said the master, "Never leave the old road for the sake of a new one."

After that they agreed for another year at the old wages, and at the end of it Ivan took instead a piece of advice, and this was it: "Never lodge where an old man is married to a young woman."

The same thing happened at the end of the third year, when the piece of advice was: "Honesty is the best policy."

But Ivan would not stay longer but wanted to go back to his wife.

"Don't go today," said his master; "my wife bakes tomorrow, and she shall make you a cake to take home to your good woman."

And when Ivan was going to leave, "Here," said his master, "here is a cake for you to take home to your wife, and, when ye are most joyous together, then break the cake, and not sooner."

So Ivan took fair leave of them and travelled towards home, and at last he came to Wayn Her, and there he met three merchants from Tre Rhyn, of his own parish, coming home from Exeter Fair.

"Oho! Ivan," said they, "come with us; glad are we to see you. Where have you been so long?"

"I have been in service," said Ivan, "and now I'm going home to my wife."

"Oh, come with us! you'll be right welcome." But when they took the new road Ivan kept to the old one. And robbers fell upon the merchants before they had gone far from Ivan as they were going by the fields of the houses in the meadow. They began to cry out, "Thieves!" and Ivan shouted out "Thieves!" too. And when the robbers heard Ivan's shout they ran away, and the merchants went by the new road and Ivan by the old one till they met again at market.

"Oh, Ivan," said the merchants, "we are beholding to you; but for you we would have been lost men. Come lodge with us at our cost, and welcome."

When they came to the place where they were to lodge, Ivan said, "I must see the host."

"The host," they cried, "what do you want with the host? Here is the hostess, and she's young and pretty. If you want to see the host, you'll find him in the kitchen."

So, Ivan went into the kitchen to see the host; he found him a weak old man turning the spit.

"Oh! oh!" said Ivan, "I'll not lodge here, but will go next door."

"Not yet," said the merchants, "sup with us, and welcome."

Now it happened that the hostess had plotted with a certain monk in the market street to murder the old man in his bed that night while the rest were asleep, and they agreed to lay it on the lodgers.

So, while Ivan was in bed next door, there was a hole in the pine-end of the house, and he saw a light through it. So, he got up and looked, and heard the monk speaking. "I had better cover this hole," said he, "or people in the next house may see our deeds." So, he stood with his back against it while the hostess killed the old man.

But meanwhile Ivan took out his knife, and putting it through the hole, cut a round piece off the monk's robe. The very next morning the hostess raised the cry that her husband was murdered, and as there was neither man nor child in the house but the merchants, she declared they ought to be hanged for it.

So, they were taken and carried to prison, till a last Ivan came to them. "Alas! alas! Ivan," cried they, "bad luck sticks to us; our host was killed last night, and we shall be hanged for it."

"Ah, tell the justices," said Ivan, "to summon the real murderers."

"Who knows," they replied, "who committed the crime?"

"Who committed the crime!" said Ivan. "If I cannot prove who committed the crime, hang me in your stead."

So, he told all he knew, and brought out the piece of cloth from the monk's robe, and with that the merchants were set at liberty, and the hostess and the monk were seized and hanged.

Then they came all together out of the market, and they said to him: "Come as far as Coed Carrn y Wylfa, the Wood of the Heap of Stones of Watching, in the parish of Burman." Then their two roads separated, and though the merchants wished Ivan to go with them, he would not go with them, but went straight home to his wife.

And when his wife saw him she said, "Home in the nick of time. Here's a purse of gold that I've found; it has no name, but sure it belongs to the great lord yonder. I was just thinking what to do when you came."

Then Ivan thought of the third counsel, and he said, "Let us go and give it to the great lord."

So, they went up to the castle, but the great lord was not in it, so they left the purse with the servant that minded the gate, and then they went home again and lived in quiet for a time.

But one day the great lord stopped at their house for a drink of water, and Ivan's wife said to him: "I hope your lordship found your lordship's purse quite safe with all its money in it."

"What purse is that you are talking about?" said the lord.

"Sure, it's your lordship's purse that I left at the castle," said Ivan.

"Come with me and we will see into the matter," said the lord.

So, Ivan and his wife went up to the castle, and there they pointed out the man to whom they had given the purse, and he had to give it up and was sent away from the castle. And the lord was so pleased with Ivan that he made him his servant in the stead of the thief.

"Honesty's the best policy!" said Ivan, as he skipped about in his new quarters. "How joyful I am!"

Then he thought of his old master's cake that he was to eat when he was most joyful, and when he broke it, to and behold, inside it was his wages for the three years he had been with him.

THE TOUCH OF CLAY

Adapted from Welsh Fairy Tales by William Elliot Griffis and originally published in 1921.

LONG, LONG AGO BEFORE THE CYMRY came into the beautiful land of Wales, there were dark-skinned people living in caves. In these early times there were a great many fairies of all sorts, but of very different kinds of behaviour, good and bad.

It was in this age of the world that fairies got an idea riveted into their heads which nothing, not even hammers, chisels or crowbars can pry up. Neither horse power, nor hydraulic force nor sixteen-inch bombs, nor cannon balls, nor torpedoes can drive it out. It is a settled matter of opinion in fairy land that, compared with fairies, human beings are very stupid. The fairies think that mortals are dull witted and awfully slow, when compared to the smarter and more nimble fairies, that are always up to date in doing things. Perhaps the following story will help explain why this is:

These ancient folks who lived in caves, could not possibly know some things that are like A B C to the fairies of today. For the Welsh fairies, King Puck and Queen Mab, know all about what is in the internets, the telegraphs, submarine cables and wireless networks of today. Puck would laugh if you should say that a telephone was any new thing to him. Long ago, in Shakespeare's time, he boasted that he could "put a girdle round the earth in forty minutes." Men have been trying ever since to catch up with him, but they have not gone ahead of him yet.

If, only three hundred years ago, this were the case, what must have been Puck's fun, when he saw men in the early days, working so hard to make even a clay cup or saucer. These people who slept and ate in cave boarding-houses, knew nothing of metals, or how to make iron or brass tools, wire, or machines, or how to touch a button and light up a whole room, which even a baby can now do.

There is one thing that we, who have travelled in many fairy lands, have often noticed and told our friends, the little folks, and that is this: All the fairies we ever knew are very slow to change either their opinions, or their ways, or their fashions. Like many mortals, they think a great deal of their own notions. They imagine that the only way to do a thing is in that which they say is the right one.

So, it came to pass that even when the Cymric folk gave up wearing the skins of animals, and put on pretty clothes woven on a loom, and ate out of dishes, instead of clam shells, there were still some fairies that kept to the notions and fashions of the cave days. To one of these, came trouble because of this failing.

Now there was once a pretty nymph, who lived in the Red Lake, to which a young and handsome farmer used to come to catch fish. One misty day, when the lad could see only a few feet before him, a wind cleared the air and blew away the fog. Then he saw near him a little old man, standing on a ladder. He was hard at work in putting a thatched roof on a hut which he had built. A few minutes later, as the mist rose and the breezes blew, the farmer could see no house, but only the ripplings of water on the lake's surface.

Although he went fishing often, he never again saw anything unusual, during the whole summer.

On one hot day in the early autumn, while he stopped to let his horse drink, he looked and saw a very lovely face on the water. Wondering to whom it might belong, there rose up before him the head and shoulders of a most beautiful woman. She was so pretty that he had two tumbles. He fell off his horse and he fell in love with her at one and the same time.

Rushing toward the lovely vision, he put out his arms at that spot where he had seen her, but only to embrace empty air. Then he remembered that love is blind. So, he rubbed his eyes, to see if he could discern anything. Yet though he peered down into the water, and up over the hills, he could not see her anywhere.

But he soon found out to his joy that his eyes were alright, for in another place, the face, flower-crowned hair, and her reflection in the water came again. Then his desire to possess the damsel was doubled. But again, she disappeared, to rise again somewhere else.

Five times he was thus tantalized and disappointed. She rose up, and quickly disappeared. It seemed as though she meant only to tease him. So, he rode home sorrowing, and scarcely slept that night.

Early morning, found the lovelorn youth again at the lake side, but for hours he watched in vain. He had left his home too excited to have eaten his usual breakfast, which greatly surprised his housekeeper. Now he pulled out some sweet apples, which a neighbour had given him, and began to munch them, while still keeping watch on the waters.

No sooner had the aroma of the apples fallen on the air, than the pretty lady of the lake bobbed up from beneath the surface, and this time quite near him. She seemed to have lost all fear, for she asked him to throw her one of the apples.

"Please come, pretty maid, and get it yourself," cried the farmer. Then he held up the red apple, turning it round and round before her, to tempt her by showing its glossy surface and rich colour.

Apparently not afraid, she came up close to him and took the apple from his left hand. At once, he slipped his strong right arm around her waist, and hugged her tight. At this, she screamed loudly. Then there appeared in the middle of the lake the old man, he had seen thatching the roof by the lake shore. This time, besides his long snowy beard, he had on his head a crown of water lilies.

"Mortal," said the venerable person. "That is my daughter you are clasping. What do you wish to do with her?"

At once, the farmer broke out in passionate appeal to the old man that she might become his wife. He promised to love her always, treat her well, and never be rough or cruel to her.

The old father listened attentively. He was finally convinced that the farmer would make a good husband for his lovely daughter. Yet he was very sorry to lose her, and he solemnly laid one condition upon his future son-in-law.

He was never under any pretence, or in any way, to strike her with clay, or with anything made or baked from clay. Any blow with that from which men made pots and pans, and jars and dishes, or in fact, with earth of any sort, would mean the instant loss of his wife. Even if children were born in their home, the mother would leave them, and return to fairy land under the lake, and be forever subject to the law of the fairies, as before her marriage.

The farmer was very much in love with his pretty prize, and as promises are easily made, he took oath that no clay should ever touch her. They were married and lived very happily together. Years passed, and the man was still a good husband and lover. He kept up the habit which he had learned from a sailor friend. Every night, when far from home and out on the sea, he and his mates used to drink this toast; "Sweethearts and wives: may every sweetheart become a wife and every wife remain a sweetheart, and every husband continue a lover."

So, he proved that though a husband he was still a lover, by always doing what she asked him and more. When the children were born and grew up, their father told them about their mother's likes and dislikes, her tastes and her wishes, and warned them always to be careful. So, it was altogether a very happy family.

One day, the wife and mother said to her husband, that she had a great longing for apples. She would like to taste some like those which he long ago gave her. At once, the good man dropped what he was doing and hurried off to his neighbour, who had first presented him with a trayful of these apples.

The farmer not only got the fruit, but he also determined that he would plant a tree and thus have apples for his wife, whenever she wanted them. So, he bought a fine young sapling, to set in his orchard, for the children to play under and to keep his pantry full of the fine red-cheeked fruit. At this his wife was delighted.

So happy enough - in fact, too merry to think of anything else, they, both husband and wife, proceeded to set the sapling in the ground. She held the tree, while he dug down to make the hole deep enough to make sure of its growing.

But farmers are sometimes very superstitious. They even believe in luck, though not in Puck. Some of them have faith in what the almanac, and the patent medicine may say, and in planting potatoes according to the moon, but they scout the idea of there being any fairies.

With the farmer, this had become a fixed state of mind and now it brought him to grief, as we shall see. For though he remembered what his wife liked and disliked, and recalled what her father had told him, he had forgotten that she was a fairy.

With this farmer and other Welsh mortals, it had become a habit, when planting a young tree, to throw the last shovelful of earth over the left shoulder. This was for good luck. The farmer was afraid to break such a good custom, as he thought it to be. So merrily he went to work, forgetting everything in his adherence to habit. He became so absorbed in his job, that he did not look where his spadeful went, and it struck his dear wife full in the breast.

At that moment, she cried out bitterly, not in pain, but in sorrow. Then she started to run towards the lake. At the shore, she called out, "Goodbye, dear, dear husband." Then, leaping into the water, she was never seen again and all his tears and those of the children never brought her back.

THE TREASURE STONE OF THE FAIRIES

Adapted from Welsh Fairy Tales by William Elliot Griffis and originally published in 1921.

THE GRUFFYDS WERE ONE OF THE largest of the Welsh tribes. Today, it is said that in Britain one man in every forty has this, as either his first, middle, or last name. It means "hero" or "brave man," and as far back as the ninth century, the word is found in the Book of Saint Chad. The monks, who derived nearly every name from the Latin, insisted the word meant Great Faith.

Another of the most common of Welsh personal names was William; which, when that of a father's son, was written Williams and was only the Latin for Gild Helm, or Golden Helmet.

Long ago, when London was a village and Cardiff only a hamlet, there was a boy of this name, who tended sheep on the hill sides. His father was a hard-working farmer, who every year tried to coax to grow out of the stony ground some oats, barley, leeks and cabbage. In summer, he worked hard, from the first croak of the raven to the last hoot of the owl, to provide food for his wife and baby daughter. When his boy was born, he took him to the church to be christened Gruffyd, but everybody called him "Gruff." In time several little sisters came to keep the boy company.

His mother always kept her cottage, which was painted pink, very neat and pretty, with vines covering the outside, while flowers bloomed indoors. These were set in pots and on shelves near the latticed windows. They seemed to grow finely, because so good a woman loved them. The copper door-sill was kept bright, and the broad borders on the clay floor, along the walls, were always fresh with whitewash. The pewter dishes on the sideboard shone as if they were moons, and the china cats on the mantelpiece, in silvery lustre, reflected both sun and candle light. Daddy often declared he could use these polished metal plates for a mirror, when he shaved his face. Puss, the pet, was always happy purring away on the hearth, as the kettle boiled to make the flummery, of sour oat jelly, which, daddy loved so well.

Mother Gruffyd was always so neat, with her black and white striped apron, her high peaked hat, with its scalloped lace and quilled fastening around her chin, her little short shawl, with its pointed, long tips, tied in a bow, and her bright red plaid petticoat folded back from her frock. Her snowy-white, rolling collar and neck cloth knotted at the top, and fringed at the ends, added fine touches to her picturesque costume. In fact, young Gruffyd was proud of his mother and he loved her dearly. He thought no woman could be quite as sweet as she was.

Once, at the end of the day, on coming back home, from the hills, the boy met some lovely children. They were dressed in very fine clothes and had elegant manners. They came up, smiled, and invited him to play with them. He joined in their sports and was too much interested to take note of time. He kept on playing with them until it was pitch dark.

Among other games, which he enjoyed, had been that of "The King in his counting house, counting out his money," and "The Queen in her kitchen, eating bread and honey," and "The Girl hanging out the clothes," and "The Saucy Blackbird that snipped off her nose." In playing these, the children had aprons full of what seemed to be real coins, the size of crowns, or five-shilling pieces, each worth a dollar. These had "head and tail," beside letters on them and the boy supposed they were real.

But when he showed these to his mother, she saw at once from their lightness, and because they were so easily bent, that they were only paper, and not silver. She asked her boy where he had got them. He told her what a nice time he had enjoyed. Then she knew that these, his playmates, were fairy children. Fearing that some evil might come of this, she charged him, her only son, never to go out again alone, on the mountain. She mistrusted that no good would come of making such strange children his companions.

But the lad was so fond of play, that one day, tired of seeing nothing but byre and garden, while his sisters liked to play girls' games more than those which boys cared most for, and the hills seeming to beckon him to come to them, he disobeyed, and slipped out and off to the mountains. He was soon missed, and search was made for him. Yet nobody had seen or heard of him. Though inquiries were made on every road, in every village, and at all the fairs and markets in the neighbourhood, two whole years passed by, without a trace of the boy.

But early one morning of the twenty-fifth month, before breakfast, his mother, on opening the door, found him sitting on the steps, with a bundle under his arm, but dressed in the same clothes, and not looking a day older or in any way different, from the very hour he disappeared.

"Why my dear boy, where have you been, all these months, which have now run into the third year? So long a time that they have seemed to me like ages?"

"Why, mother dear, how strange you talk. I left here yesterday, to go out and to play with the children, on the hills, and we have had a lovely time. See what pretty clothes they have given me for a present." Then he opened his bundle.

But when she tore open the package, the mother was all the more sure that she was right, and that her fears had been justified. In it she found only a dress of white paper. Examining it carefully, she could see neither seam nor stitches. She threw it in the fire, and again warned her son against fairy children.

But pretty soon, after a great calamity had come upon them, both father and mother changed their minds about fairies. They had put all their savings into the venture of a ship, which had for a long time made trading voyages from Cardiff. Every year, it came back bringing great profit to the owners and shareholders. In this way, daddy was able to eke out his income, and keep himself, his wife and daughters comfortably clothed, while all the time the table was well supplied with good food. Nor did they ever turn from their door anyone who asked for bread and cheese.

But in the same month of the boy's return, bad news came that the good ship had gone down in a storm. All on board had perished, and the cargo was totally lost, in the deep sea, far from land. In fact, no word except that of dire disaster had come to hand.

Now it was a tradition, as old as the days of King Arthur, that on a certain hill a great boulder could be seen, which was quite different from any other kind of rock to be found within miles. It was partly embedded in the earth, and beneath it, lay a great, yes, an untold treasure. The grass grew luxuriantly around this stone, and the sheep loved to rest at noon in its shadow. Many men had tried to lift, or pry it up, but in vain. The tradition, unaltered and unbroken for centuries, was to the effect, that none but a very good man could ever budge this stone. Any and all unworthy men might dig, or pull, or pry, until doomsday, but in vain. Till the right one came; the treasure was as safe as if in heaven.

But the boy's father and mother were now very poor, and his sisters now grown up wanted pretty clothes so badly, that the lad hoped that he or his father might be the deserving one. He would help him to win the treasure for he felt sure that his parent would share his gains with all his friends.

Though his neighbours were not told of the generous intentions credited to the boy's father, by his loving son, they all came with horses, ropes, crowbars, and tackle, to help in the enterprise. Yet after many a long days' toil, between the sun's rising and setting, their end was failure. Every day, when darkness came on, the stone lay there still, as hard and fast as ever. So, they gave up the task.

On the final night, the lad saw that father and mother, who were great lovers, were holding each other's hands, while their tears flowed together, and they were praying for patience. Seeing this, before he fell asleep, the boy resolved that on the morrow, he would go up to the mountains, and talk to his fairy friends about the matter.

So early in the morning, he hurried to the hill tops, and going into one of the caves, met the fairies and told them his troubles. Then he asked them to give him again some of their money.

"Not this time, but something better. Under the great rock there are treasures waiting for you."

"Oh, don't send me there! For all the men and horses of our parish, after working a week, have been unable to budge the stone."

"We know that," answered the principal fairy, "but do you yourself try to move it. Then you will see what is certain to happen."

Going home, to tell what he had heard, his parents had a hearty laugh at the idea of a boy succeeding where men, with the united strength of many horses and oxen, had failed. Yet, after brooding awhile, they were so dejected, that anything seemed reasonable. So they said, "Go ahead and try it."

Returning to the mountain, the fairies, in a band, went with him to the great rock. One touch of his hand, and the mighty boulder trembled, like an aspen leaf in the breeze. A shove, and the rock rolled down from the hill and crashed in the valley below. There, underneath, were little heaps of gold and silver, which the boy carried home to his parents, who became the richest people in the country round about.

THE TWO CAT WITCHES

Adapted from Welsh Fairy Tales by William Elliot Griffis and originally published in 1921.

IN OLD DAYS, IT WAS BELIEVED that the seventh son, in a family of sons, was a conjurer by nature. That is, he could work wonders like the fairies and excel the doctors in curing diseases. If he were the seventh son of a seventh son, he was himself a wonder of wonders. The story ran that he could even cure the "shingles," which is a very troublesome disease. It is called also by a Latin name, which means a snake, because, as it gets worse, it coils itself around the body.

Now the eagle can attack the serpent and conquer and kill this poisonous creature. To secure such power, Hugh, the conjurer, ate the flesh of eagles. When he wished to cure the serpent-disease, he uttered words in the form of a charm which acted as a talisman and cure. After wetting the red rash, which had broken out over the sick person's body, he muttered:

"He-eagle, she-eagle, I send you over nine seas, and over nine mountains, and over nine acres of moor and fen, where no dog shall bark, no cow low, and no eagle shall higher rise."

After that, the patient was sure that he felt better.

There was always great rivalry between these conjurers and those who made money from the Pilgrims at Holy Wells and visitors to the relic shrines, but this fellow, named Hugh, and the monks, kept on mutually good terms. They often ate dinner together, for Hugh was a great traveller over the whole country and always had news to tell to the holy brothers who lived in cells.

One night, as he was eating supper at an inn, four men came in and sat down at the table with him. By his magical power, Hugh knew that they were robbers and meant to kill him that night, in order to get his money. So, to divert their attention, Hugh made something like a horn to grow up out of the table, and then laid a spell on the robbers, so that they were kept gazing at the curious thing all night long, while he went to bed and slept soundly. When he rose in the morning, he paid his bill and went away, while the robbers were still gazing at the horn. Only when the officers arrived to take them to prison did they come to themselves.

Now at Bettws-y-Coed, that pretty place which has a name that sounds so funny to Americans and suggests a girl named Betty the Co-ed at college, there was a hotel, named the "Inn of Three Kegs." The shop sign hung out in front. It was a bunch of grapes gilded and set below three small barrels. This inn was kept by two respectable ladies, who were sisters.

Yet in that very hotel, several travellers, while they were asleep, had been robbed of their money. They could not blame anyone nor tell how the mischief was done. With the key in the keyhole, they had kept their doors locked during the night. They were sure that no one had entered the room. There were no signs of men's boots, or of anyone's footsteps in the garden, while nothing was visible on the lock or door, to show that either had been tampered with. Everything was in order as when they went to bed.

Some people doubted their stories, but when they applied to Hugh the conjurer, he believed them and volunteered to solve the mystery. His motto was "Go anywhere and everywhere but catch the thief."

When Hugh applied one night for lodging at the inn, nothing could be more agreeable than the welcome, and fine manners of his two hostesses. At supper time, and during the evening, they all chatted together merrily. Hugh, who was never at a loss for news or stories, told about the various kinds of people and the many countries he had visited, in imagination, just as if he had seen them all, though he had never set foot outside of Wales. When he was ready to go to bed, he said to the ladies, "It is my custom to keep a light burning in my room, all night, but I will not ask for candles, for I have enough to last me until sunrise." So, saying, he bade them good night.

Entering his room and locking the door, he undressed, but laid his clothes near at hand. He drew his trusty sword out of its sheath and laid it upon the bed beside him, where he could quickly grasp it. Then he pretended to be asleep and even snored. It was not long before, peeping between his eyelids, only half closed, he saw two cats come stealthily down the chimney.

When in the room, the animals frisked about, and then gambolled and romped in the liveliest way. They chased each other around the bed, as if they were trying to find out whether Hugh was asleep.

Meanwhile, the supposed sleeper kept perfectly motionless. Soon the two cats came over to his clothes and one of them put her paw into the pocket that contained his purse. At this, with one sweep of his sword, Hugh struck at the cat's paw. The beast howled frightfully, and both animals ran for the chimney and disappeared. After that, everything was quiet until breakfast time.

At the table, only one of the sisters was present. Hugh politely inquired after the other one. He was told that she was not well, for which Hugh said he was very sorry. After the meal, Hugh declared he must say goodbye to both the sisters, whose company he had so enjoyed the night before, and in spite of the other lady's many excuses, he was finally admitted to the sick lady's room to say his goodbyes.

After polite greetings and mutual compliments, Hugh offered his hand to say "goodbye." The sick lady smiled at once and put out her hand, but it was her left one. "Oh, no," said Hugh, with a laugh. "I never in all my life have taken any one's left hand, and, beautiful as yours is, I won't break my habit by beginning now and here."

Reluctantly, and as if in pain, the sick lady put out her hand. It was bandaged. The mystery was now cleared up. The two sisters were cats. By the help of bad fairies, they had changed their forms and were the real robbers.

Hugh seized the hand of the other sister and made a little cut in it, from which a few drops of blood flowed, but the spell was over. "Henceforth," said Hugh, "you are both harmless, and I trust you will both be honest women."

And they were. From that day they were like other women and kept one of the best of those inns - clean, tidy, comfortable and at modest prices - for which Wales is, or was, noted. Neither as cats with paws, nor landladies, with soaring bills, did they ever rob travellers again.

THE WELSH FAIRIES HOLD A MEETING

Adapted from Welsh Fairy Tales by William Elliot Griffis and originally published in 1921.

IN THE ANCIENT CYMRIC GATHERINGS, the Druids, poets, prophets, seers, and singers all had part. The one most honoured as the president of the meeting was crowned and garlanded. Then he was led in honour and sat in the chair of state. They called this great occasion an Eisteddfod, or sitting, after the Cymric word, meaning a chair.

All over the world, the Welsh folks, who do so passionately love music, poetry and their own grand language, hold the Eisteddfod at regular intervals. Thus, they renew their love for the Fatherland and what they received long ago from their ancestors.

Now it happens that the fairies in every land usually follow the customs of the mortals among whom they live. The Swiss, the Dutch, the Belgian, the Japanese and Korean fairies, as we all know, although they are much alike in many things are as different from each other as the countries in which they live and play. So, when the Welsh fairies all met together, they resolved to have songs and harp music and make the piper play his tunes just as in the Eisteddfod.

The Cymric fairies of our days have had many troubles to complain of. They were disgusted with so much coal smoke, the poisoning of the air by chemical fumes, and the blackening of the landscape from so many factory chimneys. They had other grievances also.

So, the Queen Mab, who had a Welsh name, and another fairy, called Pwca, or in English King Puck, sent out invitations into every part of Wales, for a gathering on the hills, near the great rock called Dina's seat. This is a rocky chair formed by nature. They also included in their call those parts of western and south England, such as are still Welsh and spiritually almost a part of Wales. In fact, Cornwall was the old land, in which the Cymry had first landed when coming from over the sea.

The meeting was to be held on a moonlight night, and far away from any houses, lest the merrymaking, dancing and singing of the fairies should keep the farmers awake. This was something of which the yokels, or men of the plough, often complained. They could not sleep while the fairies were having their parties.

Now among the Welsh fairies of every sort, size, dress, and behaviour, some were good, others were bad, but most of them were only full of fun and mischief. Chief of these was the lively little fellow, Puck, who lived in Cwm Pwcca, that is, Puck Valley, in Breconshire.

It had been an old custom, which had come down, from the days of the cave men, that when anyone died, the people, friends and relatives sat up all night with the corpse. The custom arose, at first, with the idea of protection against wild beasts and later from insult by enemies. This was called a wake. The watchers wept and wailed at first, and then fell to eating and drinking. Sometimes, they got to be very lively. The young folks even looked on a wake, after the first hour or two, as fine fun. Strong liquor was too plentiful, and it often happened that quarrels broke out. When heads were thus fuddled, men saw or thought they saw, many uncanny things, like leather birds, cave eagles, and the like.

But all these fantastic things and creatures, such as foolish people talk about, and with which they frighten children, such as corpse candles, demons and imps, were ruled out and not invited to the fairy meeting. Some other objects, which ignorant folks believed in, were not to be allowed in the company. The door-keeper was notified not to admit the eagles of darkness, that live in a cave which is never lighted up; or the weird, featherless bird of leather, from the Land of Illusion and Phantasy, that brushes its wing against windows, when a funeral is soon to take place; or the greedy dog with silver eyes. None of these would be permitted to show themselves, even if they came and tried to get in. Some other creatures, not recognized in the good society of Fairyland, were also barred out.

To this gathering, only the bright and lively fairies were welcome. Some of the best natured among the big creatures, and especially giants and dragons, might pay a visit, if they wanted to do so; but all the bad ones, such as lake hags, wraiths, sellers of liquids for wakes, who made men drunk, and all who, under the guise of fairies, were only agents for undertakers, were ruled out. The Night Dogs of the Wicked Hunter Annum, the monster Afang, Cadwallader's Goats, and various, cruel goblins and ogres, living in the ponds, and that pulled cattle down to eat them up, and the immodest mermaids, whose bad behaviour was so well known, were crossed off the list of invitations.

No ugly brats, such as wicked fairies were in the habit of putting in the cradles of mortal mothers, when they stole away their babies, were allowed to be present, even if they should come with their mothers. This was to be a perfectly respectable company, and no bawling, squealing, crying, or blubbering was to be permitted.

When they had all gathered together, at the evening hour, there was seen, in the moonlight, the funniest lot of creatures, that one could imagine, but all were neatly dressed and well behaved. Quite a large number of the famous Fair Family, that moved only in the best society of fairyland, fathers, mothers, cousins, uncles and aunts, were on hand. In fact, some of them had thought it was to be a wake, and were ready for whatever might turn up, whether solemn or frivolous. These were dressed in varied costume.

Queen Mab, who above all else, was a Welsh fairy, and whose name, as everybody knows who talks Cymric, suggested her extreme youth and lively disposition, was present in all her glory. When they saw her, several learned fairies, who had come from a distance, fell at once into conversation on this subject. One remarked: "How would the Queen like to add another syllable to her name? Then we should call her Mab-gath (which means Kitten, or Little Puss)."

"Well not so bad, however; because many mortal daddies, who have a daughter, call her Puss. It is a term of affection with them and the little girls never seem to be offended."

"Oh! Suppose that in talking to each other we call our Queen Mab-gar, what then?" asked another, with a roguish twinkle in the eye.

"It depends on how you use it," said a wise one dryly. This fairy was a stickler for the correct use of every word. "If you meant 'babyish,' or 'childish,' she, or her friends might demur; but, if you use the term 'love of children,' what better name for a fairy queen?"

"None. There could not be any," they shouted, all at once, "but let us ask our old friend the harper."

Now such a thing as inquiring into each other's ages was not common in Fairy Land. Very few ever asked such a question, for it was not thought to be polite. For, though we hear of ugly fairy brats being put into the cradles, in place of pretty children, no one ever heard, either of fairies being born or of dying, or having clocks, or watches, or looking to see what time it was. Nor did doctors, or the census clerks, or directory people ever trouble the fairy ladies, to ask their age.

Occasionally, however, there was one fairy, so wise, so learned, and so able to tell what was going to happen tomorrow, or next year, that the other fairies looked up to such a one with respect and awe.

Yet these honourable would hardly know what you were talking about, if you asked any of them how old they might be, or spoke of "old" or "young." If, by any chance, a fairy did use the world "old" in talking of their number, it would be for honour or dignity, and they would mean it for a compliment.

The fact was, that many of the liveliest fairies showed their frivolous disposition at once. These were of the kind, that, like kittens, cubs, or babies, wanted to play all the time, yes, every moment. Already, hundreds of them were tripping from flower to flower, riding on the backs of fireflies, or harnessing night moths, or any winged creatures they could saddle, for flight through the air. Or, they were waltzing with glow worms, or playing "ring around a rosy," or dancing in circles. They could not keep still, one moment.

In fact, when a great crowd of the frolicsome creatures got singing together, they made such a noise, that a squad of fairy policemen, dressed in club moss and armed with pistols, was sent to warn them not to raise their voices too high; lest the farmers, especially those that were kind to the fairies, should be awakened, and feel in bad humour.

So the knot of learned fairies had a quiet time to talk, and, when able to hear their own words, the harper, who was very learned, answered their questions about Queen Mab as follows: "Well, you know the famous children's story book, in which mortals read about us, and which they say they enjoy so much, is named Mabinogion, that is, The Young Folks' Treasury of Cymric Stories."

"It is well named," said another fairy savant, "since Queen Mab is the only fairy that waits on men. She inspires their dreams, when these are born in their brains."

The talk now turned on Puck, who was to be the president of the meeting. They were expected to show much dignity in his presence, but some feared he would, as usual, play his pranks. Before he arrived in his chariot, which was drawn by dragon flies, some of his neighbours that lived in the valley nearby chatted about him, until the gossip became quite personal. Just for the fun of it, and the amusement of the crowd, they wanted Puck to give an exhibition, off-hand, of all his very varied accomplishments for he could beat all rivals in his special variety, or as musicians say, his repertoire.

"No. 'Twould be too much like a Merry Andrew's or a Buffoon's sideshow, where the freaks of all sorts are gathered, such as they have at those county fairs, which the mortals get up, to which are gathered great crowds. The charge of admission is a sixpence. I vote 'no.'"

"Well, for the very reason that Puck can beat the rest of us at spells and transformations, I should like to see him do for us as many stunts as he can. I've heard from a mortal, named Shakespeare, that, in one performance, Puck could be a horse, a hound, a hog, a bear without any head, and even kindle himself into a fire; while his vocal powers, as we know, are endless. He can neigh, bark, grunt, roar, and even burn up things. Now, I should like to see the fairy that could beat him at tricks. It was Puck himself, who told the world that he was in the habit of doing all these things, and I want to see whether he was boasting."

"Tut, tut, don't talk that way, about our king," said a fourth fairy.

All this was only chaff and fun, for all the fairies were in good humour. They were only talking, to fill up the interval until the music began.

Now the canny Welsh fairies had learned the trick of catching farthings, pennies and sixpences from the folks who have more curiosity in them than even fairies do. These human beings, cunning fellows that they are, let the curtain fall on a show, just at the most interesting part. Then they tell you to come next day and find out what is to happen. Or, as they say in a story paper, "to be continued in our next." Or, worse than all, the storyteller stops, at some very exciting episode, and then passes the hat or collection-box around, to get the copper or silver of his listeners, before he will go on.

This time, however, it was Puck himself who came forward and declared that, unless every one of the fairies would promise to attend the next meeting, there should be no music. Now a meeting of the Welshery, whether fairies or human, without music was a thing not to be thought of. So, although at first some fairies grumbled and held back, and were quite sulky about it, even muttering other grumpy words, they at last all agreed, and Puck sent for the fiddler to make music for the dance.

WELSH RABBIT AND HUNTED HARES

Adapted from Welsh Fairy Tales by William Elliot Griffis and originally published in 1921.

LONG, LONG AGO, THERE WAS A good saint named David, who taught the early Cymric or Welsh people better manners and many good things to eat and ways of enjoying themselves. Now the Welsh folks in speaking of their good teacher pronounced his name Tafid and affectionately Taffy, and this came to be the usual name for a person born in Wales. In good Welsh nurseries children learned that "Taffy was a Welshman," but it was their enemies who made a bad rhyme about Taffy.

Wherever there were cows or goats, people could get milk. So, they always had what was necessary for a good meal, whether it was breakfast, dinner or supper. Milk, cream, curds, whey and cheese enriched the family table. Were not these enough?

But Saint David taught the people how to make a still more delicious food out of cheese, and that this could be done without taking the life of any creature.

Saint David showed the girls how to take cheese, slice and toast it over the coals, or melt it in a skillet and pour it hot over toast or biscuit. This gave the cheese a new and sweeter flavour. When spread on bread, either plain, or browned over the fire, the result, in combination, was a delicacy fit for a king, and equal to anything known.

The fame of this new addition to the British bill of fare spread near and far. The English people, who had always been fond of rabbit pie, and still eat thousands of Molly Cotton Tails every day, named it "Welsh Rabbit," and thought it one of the best things to eat. In fact, there are many people, who do not easily see a joke, who misunderstand the fun, or who suppose the name to be either slang, or vulgar, or a mistake, and who call it "rarebit." It is like "Cape Cod turkey", which is really codfish, or "Bombay ducks", which are really dried fish, or "Irish plums", which are potatoes, and such funny cookery with fancy names.

Now up to this time, the rabbits and hares had been so hunted with the aid of dogs, that there was hardly a chance of any of them surviving the cruel slaughter.

In the year 604, the Prince of Powys was out hunting. The dogs started a hare and pursued it into a dense thicket. When the hunter with the horn came up, a strange sight met his eyes. There he saw a lovely maiden. She was kneeling on the ground and devoutly praying. Though surprised at this, the prince was anxious to secure his game. He hissed on the hounds and ordered the horn to be blown, for the dogs to charge on their prey, expecting them to bring him the game at once. Instead of this, though they were trained dogs and would fight even a wolf, they slunk away howling, and frightened, as if in pain, while the horn stuck fast to the lips of the blower and he was silent. Meanwhile, the hare nestled under the maiden's dress and seemed not in the least disturbed.

Amazed at this, the prince turned to the fair lady and asked, "Who are you?"

She answered, "My mother named me Monacella. I have fled from Ireland, where my father wished to marry me to one of his chief men, whom I did not love. Under God's guidance, I came to this secret deserted place, where I have lived for fifteen years, without seeing the face of man."

To this, the prince in admiration replied, "O most worthy Melangell [which is the way the Welsh pronounce Monacella], because, on account of your merits, it has pleased God to shelter and save this little, wild hare, I, on my part, herewith present you with this land, to be for the service of God and an asylum for all men and women, who seek your protection. So long as they do not pollute this sanctuary, let none, not even prince or chieftain, drag them forth."

The beautiful saint passed the rest of her life in this place. At night, she slept on the bare rock. Many were the wonders wrought for those who with pure hearts sought her refuge. The little wild hares were under her special protection, and they are still called "Melangell's Lambs."

WHY THE BACKDOOR WAS FRONT

Adapted from Welsh Fairy Tales by William Elliot Griffis and originally published in 1921.

IN THE DAYS WHEN THERE WERE no books, or writing, and folk tales were the only ones told, there was an old woman, who had a bad reputation. She pretended to be very poor, so as not to attract or tempt robbers. Yet those who knew her best, knew also, as a subject of common talk, that she was always counting out her coins.

Besides this, she lived in a nice house, and it was believed that she made a living by stealing babies out of their cradles to sell to the bad fairies. It was matter of rumour that she would, for an extra-large sum, take a wicked fairy's ugly brat, and put it in place of a mother's darling. In addition to these horrid charges against her, it was rumoured that she laid a spell, or charm, on the cattle of people whom she did not like, in order to take revenge on them.

The old woman denied all this, and declared it was only silly gossip of envious people who wanted her money. She lived so comfortably, she averred, because her son, who was a stonemason, who made much money by building chimneys, which had then first come into fashion. When he brought to her the profits of his jobs, she counted the coins, and because of this, some people were jealous, and told bad stories about her. She declared she was thrifty, but neither a miser, nor a kidnaper, nor a witch.

One day, this old woman wanted more feathers to stuff into her bed, to make it softer and feel pleasanter for her old bones to rest upon, for what she slept on was nearly worn through. So, she went to a farm, where they were plucking geese, and asked for a few handfuls of feathers. But the rich farmer's people refused and ordered her out of the farm yard.

Shortly after this event, the cows of this farmer, who was opposed to chimneys, and did not like her or her son, suffered dreadfully from the disease called the black quarter. As they had no horse doctors or professors of animal economy, or veterinarians in those days, many of the cows died. The rich farmer lost much money, for he had now no milk or beef to sell. At once, he suspected that his cattle were bewitched, and that the old woman had cast a spell on them. In those days, it was very easy to think so.

So, the angry man went one day to the old crone, when she was alone, and her stout son was away on a distant job. He told her to remove the charm, which she had laid on his beasts, or he would tie her arms and legs together, and pitch her into the river.

The old woman denied vehemently that she possessed any such powers or had ever practiced such black arts.

To make sure of it, the farmer made her say out loud, "The Blessing of God be upon your cattle!" To clinch the matter, he compelled her to repeat the Lord's Prayer, which she was able to do, without missing one syllable. She used the form of words which are not found in the prayer book, but are in the Bible, and was very earnest, when she prayed "Forgive us our debts, as we forgive our debtors."

But after all that trouble, and the rough way which the rich farmer took to save his cattle, his efforts were in vain. In spite of that kind of religion which he professed, which was shown by bullying a poor old woman, his cattle were still sick, with no sign of improvement. He was at his wits' end to know what to do next.

Now, as we have said, this was about the time that chimneys came into fashion. In very old days, the Cymric house was a round hut, with a thatched roof, without glass windows, and the smoke got out through the door and holes in the walls, in the best way it could. The only tapestry in the hut was in the shape of long festoons of soot, that hung from the roof or rafters. These, when the wind blew, or the fire was lively, would swing or dance or whirl, and often fall on the heads, or into the food, while the folks were eating. When the children cried, or made wry faces at the black stuff, their daddy only laughed, and said it was healthy, or was for good luck.

But by and by, the carpenters and masons made much improvement, especially when, instead of flint hatchets, they had iron axes and tools. Then they hewed down trees, that had thick cross branches and set up columns in the centre and made timber walls and rafters. Then the house was square or oblong. In other words, the Cymric folks squared the circle.

Now they began to have lattices, and, much later, even glass windows. They removed the fireplace from the middle of the floor and set it at the end of the house, opposite the door, and built chimneys. Then they set the beds at the side and made sleeping rooms. This was done by stretching curtains between partitions. They had also a loft, in which to keep odds and ends. They hung up the bacon and hams, and strings of onions, and made a mantlepiece over the fireplace. They even began to decorate the walls with pictures and to set pewter dishes, china cats, and Dresden shepherds in rows on the shelves for ornaments.

Now people wore shoes and the floor, instead of being muddy, or dusty, with pools and puddles of water in the time of rainy weather and with the pigs and chickens running in and out, was of clay, beaten down flat and hard, and neatly whitewashed at the edges. Outside, in front, were laid nice flat flagstones, that made a pleasant path to the front door. Flowers, inside and out, added to the beauty of the home and made perfume for those who loved them.

The rich farmer had just left his old round hut and now lived in one of the new and better kind of houses. He was very proud of his chimney, which he had built higher than any of his neighbours, but he could not be happy, while so many of his cows were sick or dying. Besides, he was envious of other people's prosperity and cared nothing, when they, too, suffered.

One night, while he was standing in front of his fine house and wondering why he must be vexed with so many troubles, he talked to himself and, speaking out loud, said, "Why don't my cows get well?"

"I'll tell you," said a voice behind him. It seemed half way between a squeak and a growl.

He turned around and there he saw a little, angry man. He was dressed in red and stood hardly as high as the farmer's knee. The little old man glared at the big fellow and cried out in a high tone of voice, "You must change your habits of disposing of your garbage, for other people have chimneys besides you."

"What has that to do with sickness among my cows?"

"Much indeed. Your family is the cause of your troubles, for they throw all their slops down my chimney and put out my fire."

The farmer was puzzled beyond the telling, for he owned all the land within a mile, and knew of no house in sight.

"Put your foot on mine, and then you will have the power of vision, to see clearly," said the angry little man.

The farmer's big boot was at once placed on the little man's slipper, and when he looked down he almost laughed at the contrast in size. What was his real surprise, when he saw that the slops thrown out of his house, did actually fall down; and, besides, the contents of the full bucket, when emptied, kept on dripping into the chimney of a house which stood far below, but which he had never seen before. But as soon as he took his foot off that of the tiny little man, he saw nothing. Everything like a building vanished as in a dream.

"I see that my family have done wrong and injured yours. Pray forgive me. I'll do what I can to make amends for it."

"It's no matter now, if you only do as I ask you. Shut up your front door, build a wall in its place, and then my family will not suffer from yours."

The rich farmer thought all this was very funny, and he had a hearty laugh over it all. Yet he did exactly as the little man in the red cloak had so politely asked him. He walled up the old door at the front, and built another at the back of the house, which opened out into the garden. Then he made the path, on which to go in from the roadway to the threshold, around the corners and over a longer line of flagstones. Then he removed the fireplace and chimney to what had been the front side of the house but was now the back. For the next thing, he had a copper door sill nailed down, which his housemaid polished, until it shone as bright as gold.

Yet long before this, his cows had got well, and they now gave more and richer milk than ever. He became the wealthiest man in the district. His children all grew up to be fine looking men and women. His grandsons were famous engineers and introduced paving and drainage in the towns so that today, for both man and beast, Wales is one of the healthiest of countries.

WILLIAM DAVIES

Adapted from Welsh Folk-Lore by Owain Elias, published in 1896 by Woodall, Minshall and Co, and based on Elias' prize essay of the national Eisteddfod, 1887.

WILLIAM DAVIES, OF PENRHIW, NEAR Aberystwyth, went to England for the harvest, and after having worked there about three weeks, he returned home alone, with all possible haste, as he knew that his father-in-law's fields were by this time ripe for the sickle. He, however, failed to accomplish the journey before Sunday; but he determined to travel on Sunday, and thus reach home on Sunday night to be ready to commence reaping on Monday morning.

His conscience, though, would not allow him to be at rest, but he endeavoured to silence its twittings by saying to himself that he had with him no clothes to go to a place of worship. He stealthily, therefore, walked on, feeling very guilty every step he took, and dreading to meet anyone going to chapel or church.

By Sunday evening he had reached the hill overlooking Llanfihangel Creuddyn, where he was known, so he determined not to enter the village until after the people had gone to their respective places of worship; he therefore sat down on the hill side and contemplated the scene below. He saw the people leave their houses for the house of God, he heard their songs of praise, and that was when he thought he could venture to descend and pass through the village unobserved. Luckily no one saw him going through the village.

William entered a barley field, and although still uneasy in mind, he felt somewhat reassured, and stepped on quickly. He had not proceeded far in the barley field before he found himself surrounded by a large number of small pigs. He was not much struck by this, though he thought it strange that so many pigs should be allowed to wander about on the Sabbath day. The pigs, however, came up to him, stared at him, grunted, and scampered away.

Before he had traversed the barley field he saw approaching him an innumerable number of mice, and these, too, surrounded him, only, however, to stare at him, and then to disappear. By this Davies began to be frightened, and he was almost sorry that he had broken the Sabbath day by travelling with his pack on his back instead of keeping the day holy.

He was not now very far from home, and this thought gave him courage and on he went. He had not proceeded any great distance from the spot where the mice had appeared when he saw a large greyhound walking before him on the pathway. He anxiously watched the dog, but suddenly it vanished out of his sight. By this the poor man was thoroughly frightened, and many and truly sincere were his regrets that he had broken the Sabbath; but on he went.

He passed through the village of Llanilar without any further fright. He had now gone about three miles from Llanfihangel along the road that goes to Aberystwyth, and he had begun to dispel the fear that had seized him, but to his horror he saw something approach him that made his hair stand on end. He could not at first make it out, but he soon clearly saw that it was a horse that was madly dashing towards him. He had only just time to step on to the ditch, when, horrible to relate, a headless white horse rushed past him. His limbs shook, and the perspiration stood out like beads on his forehead. This terrible spectre he saw when close to Tan'rallt, but he dared not turn into the house, as he was travelling on Sunday, so on he went again, and heartily did he wish himself at home.

In fear and dread he proceeded on his journey towards Penrhiw. The most direct way from Tan'rallt to Penrhiw was a pathway through the fields, and Davies took this pathway, and now he was in sight of his home, and he hastened towards the boundary fence between Tan'rallt and Penrhiw. He knew that there was a gap in the hedge that he could get through, and for this gap he aimed; he reached it, but further progress was impossible, for in the gap was a lady lying at full length, and immovable, and stopping up the gap entirely.

Poor Davies was now more thoroughly terrified than ever. He sprang aside, he screamed, and then he fainted right away. As soon as he recovered consciousness, he, on his knees, and in a loud supplicating voice, prayed for pardon. His mother and father-in-law heard him, and the mother knew the voice and said, "It is my Will; some mishap has overtaken him." They went to him and found he was so weak that he could not move, and they were obliged to carry him home, where he recounted to them his marvellous experience.

A local reverend gentleman, who was intimately acquainted with William Davies, had many conversations with him about his Sunday journey, and he argued the matter with him, and tried to persuade William that he had seen nothing, but that it was his imagination working on a nervous temperament that had created all his fantasies. He however failed to convince him, for William affirmed that it was no hallucination, but that what he had seen that Sunday was a punishment for his having broken the Fourth Commandment. It need hardly be added that Davies ever afterwards was a strict observer of the Day of Rest.

Y FUWCH GYFEILIORN

*Adapted from Welsh Folk-Lore by Owain Elias, published in 1896
by Woodall, Minshall and Co, and based on Elias' prize essay of
the national Eisteddfod, 1887.*

A SHREWD OLD HILL FARMER BY the name of Thomas
Abergroes, well skilled in the folk-lore of the district, informed
Owain Elias that, in years gone by, though when, exactly, he was
too young to remember, the Gwragedd Annwn (Annwn Women)
were wont to make their appearance, arrayed in green, in the
neighbourhood of Llyn Barfog, chiefly at eventide, accompanied
by their cows and hounds, and that, on quiet summer nights in
particular, these ban-hounds were often to be heard in full cry,
pursuing their prey along the upland township of Cefn Rhos Uchaf.
Their prey were the souls of doomed men dying without baptism
and penance.

Many a farmer had a sight of their comely, milk-white cows; many
a swain had his soul turned to romance and poesy by a sudden
vision of themselves in the guise of damsels arrayed in green, and
radiant in beauty and grace; and many a sportsman had his path
crossed by the white hounds of supernatural fleetness and
comeliness, the Cwn Annwn (Annwn Dogs); but never had anyone
been favoured with more than a passing view of either, till an old

farmer of Dyssyrnant, in the adjoining valley of Dyffryn Gwyn, became at last the lucky captor of one of their milk-white cows.

The acquaintance which the Gwartheg y Llyn, the cows of the lake, had formed with the farmer's cattle, like the loves of the angels for the daughters of men, became the means of capture; and the farmer was thereby enabled to add the mystic cow to his own herd, an event in all cases believed to be most conducive to the worldly prosperity of him who should make so fortunate an acquisition. Never was there such a cow, never were there such calves, never such milk and butter, or cheese; and the fame of the Fuwch Gyfeiliorn, the stray cow, was soon spread abroad through that central part of Wales known as the district of Rhwng y ddwy Afon, from the banks of the Mawddach to those of the Dofwy, and from Aberdiswnwy to Abercorris.

The farmer, from a small beginning, rapidly became, like Job, a man of substance, possessed of thriving herds of cattle, and grew in stature to become a patriarch among the mountains. But, alas! wanting Job's restraining grace, his wealth made him proud, his pride made him forget his obligation to the elfin cow and fearing she might soon become too old to be profitable, he fattened her for the butcher, and then even she did not fail to distinguish herself, for a more monstrously fat beast was never seen.

At last the day of slaughter came, which is an eventful day in the annals of a mountain farm, especially with the killing of a fat cow, and such a monster of obesity. No wonder all the neighbours were gathered together to see the sight. The old farmer looked upon the preparations in self-pleased importance; the butcher felt he was about no common feat of his craft, and, baring his arm, he struck the first blow.

But the blow was never fatal, for before even a hair had been injured, his arm was paralysed, the knife dropped from his hand, and the whole company was electrified by a piercing cry that awakened an echo in a dozen hills and made the welkin ring again; and lo and behold! the whole assemblage saw a female figure, clad in green, with uplifted arms, standing on one of the rocks overhanging Llyn Barfog, and heard her calling with a voice loud as thunder:

Come you Einion's yellow one,

Stray horns - speckled one of the Lake,

And the hornless Dodin,

Arise, come home.

And no sooner were these words of power uttered than the original lake cow, and all her progeny to the third and fourth generations, were in full flight towards the heights of Llyn Barfog, as if pursued by the evil one.

Self-interest quickly roused the farmer, who followed in pursuit, till, breathless and panting, he gained an eminence overlooking the lake, but with no better success than to behold the green-attired dame leisurely descending mid-lake, accompanied by the fugitive cows, and her calves formed in a circle around her. They tossed their tails, and she waved her hands in scorn, as much as to say, "You may catch us, my friend, if you can," as they disappeared beneath the dark waters of the lake, leaving only the yellow water-lily to mark the spot where they vanished, and to perpetuate the memory of this strange event.

Meanwhile, the farmer looked with rueful countenance upon the spot where the elfin herd disappeared, and had ample leisure to deplore the effects of his greediness, as with them also departed the prosperity which had hitherto attended him, and he became impoverished to a degree below his original circumstances, and in his altered circumstances few felt pity for one who, in the noontide flow of prosperity, had shown himself so far forgetful of favours received, as to purpose slaying his benefactor.

HISTORICAL NOTES

This section contains some brief biographical notes about the original collectors and their books featured in this collection. These notes have been adapted from those primarily on Wikipedia along with other supporting sources and notes.

William Elliot Griffis

William Elliot Griffis, 1843–1928, was an American orientalist, Congregational minister, lecturer, and prolific author.

Griffis was born in Philadelphia, Pennsylvania, the son of a sea captain and coal trader. During the American Civil War, he served two months as a corporal in Company H of the 44th Pennsylvania Militia after Robert E. Lee invaded Pennsylvania in 1863. After the war, he attended Rutgers University at New Brunswick, New Jersey, graduating in 1869. At Rutgers, Griffis was an English and Latin language tutor for Tarō Kusakabe, a young samurai from the Japanese province of Echizen.

After a year of travel in Europe, he studied at the seminary of the Reformed Church in America in New Brunswick, but in 1903 he resigned from the active ministry to devote himself exclusively to writing and lecturing. His books on Japan and Japanese culture were complemented with extensive college and university lecture circuit itineraries. In addition to his own books and articles during this period, he also joined Inazo Nitobe in crafting what became his most well-known book, *Bushido: The Soul of Japan*.

In 1907, the Japanese government conferred the Order of the Rising Sun, Gold Rays with Rosette, which represents the fourth highest of eight classes associated with the award.

The prolific writer was also a prolific traveller, making eleven trips to Europe - primarily to visit the Netherlands. In 1898, he was present at the enthronement of Queen Wilhelmina, and he attended the Congress of Diplomatic History. He was among the group of Bostonians who wanted to commemorate the Pilgrims' roots in Holland, and the work was rewarded with the dedication of a memorial at Delfshaven and the placement of five other bronze historical tablets in 1909. He was one of four Americans elected to the Netherlands Society of Letters in Leiden.

In 1923 Griffis published *The Story of the Walloons: At Home in Lands of Exile and in America*. In this work he reveals the long history and contributions of these Belgians. The last half of the book relates the story of New Belgium (Nova Belgica) in America, the first settlers of Manhattan being a group of Protestant Walloons who petitioned the Dutch West India Company to be sent to establish a colony in the New World.

In 1926, Griffis was invited to return to Japan; and on this trip, the Japanese government conferred a second decoration. He was presented with the Order of the Rising Sun, Gold Rays with Neck Ribbon, which represents the third highest of eight classes.

Griffis was a founding member of the National Institute of Arts and Letters (later to become the American Academy of Arts and Letters), the American Historical Association, and the U.S. Naval Institute. He died at his winter home in Florida in 1928.

Joseph Jacobs

Joseph Jacobs, 1854–1916, was an Australian folklorist, translator, literary critic, social scientist, historian and writer of English literature who became a notable collector and publisher of English folklore.

Jacobs was born in Sydney. His work went on to popularise some of the world's best known versions of English fairy tales including *Jack and the Beanstalk, Goldilocks and the three bears, The Three Little Pigs, Jack the Giant Killer* and *The History of Tom Thumb*. He published his English fairy tale collections: *English Fairy Tales* in 1890 and *More English Fairy Tales* in 1893, but also went on after and in between both books to publish fairy tales collected from continental Europe as well as Jewish, Celtic and Indian fairy tales which made him one of the most popular writers of fairy tales for the English language.

Jacobs was also an editor for journals and books on the subject of folklore which included editing the *Fables of Bidpa*i and the *Fables of Aesop*, as well as articles on the migration of Jewish folklore. He also edited editions of *The Thousand and One Nights*. He went on to join The Folklore Society in England and became an editor of the society journal Folklore. Joseph Jacobs also contributed to *The Jewish Encyclopaedia*.

During his lifetime, Jacobs came to be regarded as one of the foremost experts on English folklore.

In 1896, Jacobs visited the United States to deliver his lectures on *The Philosophy of Jewish History* to Gratz College in Philadelphia and to groups of the Council of Jewish Women at New York, Philadelphia, and Chicago. In 1900, he was invited to serve as revising editor for the *Jewish Encyclopaedia*, which included entries from 600 contributors. He moved to the United States to take on this task. There he involved himself in the American Jewish Historical Society. He became a working member of the Jewish Publication Society's publication committee.

Jacobs married Georgina Horne and fathered two sons and a daughter. In 1900, when he became revising editor of the *Jewish Encyclopaedia*, based in New York, he settled permanently in the United States.

He died on 30 January 1916 at his home in Yonkers, New York, aged 62.

Owain Elias

The Reverend Elias Owen MA, F.S.A.,1833-1899) was a Welsh cleric and antiquarian whose works include *The Old Stone Crosses of the Vale of Clwyd*, 1886 and *Welsh Folk-Lore*, 1896.

He was born in Montgomeryshire, probably in the village of Llandysilio, the third child and eldest son of James Owen and Susannah Morgan. His father was a farmer and one of the first 12 constables in the Montgomeryshire Constabulary. Elias Owen married Margaret Pierce in 1858 at St. David's Church, the Welsh chapel in Brownlow Hill, Liverpool

During his years as a school inspector, Owen travelled extensively in Wales visiting and inspecting schools. It was his custom, after the labour of school inspection was over, to ask the clergy with whom he was staying to accompany him to the most aged inhabitants of their parish. This they willingly did, and often in the dark winter evenings, lantern in hand, they sallied forth on their journey, and in this way a rich deposit of traditions and superstitions was struck and rescued from oblivion.

In this way he collected a vast amount of material which he was able to supplement with material supplied by his brother Elijah, who was a vicar in Anglesey, and several other churchmen. This material was assembled by Owen and formed the basis of an essay he presented to the 1887 Welsh National Eisteddfod, held in London. The essay won a prize of a silver medal and £20. The essay was later revised and published under the title *Welsh Folk-Lore. A Collection of the Folk-Tales and Legends of North Wales* in 1896.

Owen died on 19 May 1899, aged 65 while he was at work in his smoking room at Llanyblodwel on The Holy Wells of North Wales. Owen is commemorated in the church of St. Michael the Archangel at Llanyblodwel with a stained glass window of the Good Shepherd and St Michael. His gravestone bears the inscription: "We all do fade as a leaf".(Isaiah 64:6)

William Wirt Sikes

William Wirt Sikes was born in Watertown, New York, the son of William Johnson Sikes, a prominent local physician. He was the seventh of eleven children, of whom only six survived to adulthood. Sikes himself was seriously ill as a child and almost lost his hearing, so he was largely educated at home. At fourteen he went to work for a printer and learned how to set type. He supported himself thereafter by typesetting, contributing to local newspapers, and giving temperance lectures.

At the age of nineteen, on August 28, 1855, he married Jeannette Annie Wilcox, and they had two children, George Preston Sikes and Clara Jeanette Sikes.

By 1856 he was working at the Utica Morning Herald as a typesetter and contributor. He published a book of stories and poems, *A Book for the Winter-Evening Fireside*, in 1858. He spent time in Chicago working at newspapers there, and around 1860 worked on a paper called City and Country in Nyack, New York. In 1862 he was given the job of canal inspector in Chicago for the state-owned Illinois and Michigan Canal. While in Chicago he was separated from his wife, by mutual consent, and they divorced in 1870.

Between 1865 and 1867 he went to New York City to work on newspapers. He continued to write, publishing stories in The Youth's Companion, Oliver Optic's Magazine, and others. He published two novels, *The World's Broad Stage* and *One Poor Girl* (1869). Sikes gave lectures and was represented by the Boston Lyceum Bureau from 1869–71. He married fellow lecturer Olive Logan on December 19, 1871.

After their marriage the couple went to Europe, where they continued to practice journalism. Sikes produced a biographical and critical piece on the Wiertz Museum for Harper's Magazine in 1873 which was later reprinted by the museum.

In June 1876 Sikes was appointed U.S. Consul at Cardiff, Wales. Over the next few years Sikes produced a number of pieces on Welsh folklore, mythology, and customs, collected as *British Goblins; Welsh Folk-Lore, Fairy Mythology, Legends, and Traditions* (1880) and *Rambles and Studies in Old South Wales* (1881). He also wrote *Studies of Assassination* (1881). He died in

Cardiff in 1883 and was buried in Brookwood Cemetery, Brookwood, Surrey.

Sikes is said to have used as many as thirty pseudonyms for his prolific output, as well as material published under his own name. As "Burton Saxe" he wrote the dime novel *The Black Hunter; or, The Cave Secret* (American Tales #22, 1865).

In George Presbury Rowell's memoir *Forty Years an Advertising Agent*, he recalls a column in the New York Tribune, "wherein certain literary characters were reviewed in grades and classes, beginning with - I don't remember whom, Thackeray perhaps, and descending, as the editor expressed it, 'down to Wirt Sikes'".

Peter Henry Emerson

Peter Henry Emerson, 1856–1936) was a British writer and photographer. His photographs are early examples of promoting photography as an art form. He is known for taking photographs that displayed natural settings and for his disputes with the photographic establishment about the purpose and meaning of photography.

Emerson was born on La Palma Estate, a sugar plantation near Encrucijada, Cuba, belonging to his American father, Henry Ezekiel Emerson and British mother, Jane. He was a distant relative of Samuel Morse and Ralph Waldo Emerson. He spent his early years in Cuba on his father's estate. During the American Civil War he spent some time at Wilmington, Delaware, but moved to England in 1869, after the death of his father. He was schooled at Cranleigh School where he was a noted scholar and athlete. He subsequently attended King's College London, before switching to

Clare College, Cambridge in 1879 where he earned his medical degree in 1885.

In 1881 he married Miss Edith Amy Ainsworth and wrote his first book while on his honeymoon. The couple eventually had five children.

He bought his first camera around 1881 to be used as a tool on bird-watching trips with his friend, the ornithologist A. T. Evans. In 1885 he was involved in the formation of the Camera Club of London, and the following year he was elected to the Council of the Photographic Society and abandoned his career as a surgeon to become a photographer and writer. As well as his particular attraction to nature he was also interested in billiards, rowing and meteorology.

Initially influenced by naturalistic French painting, he argued for similarly "naturalistic" photography and took photographs in sharp focus to record country life as clearly as possible. His first album of photographs, published in 1886, was entitled *Life and Landscape on the Norfolk Broads*, and it consisted of 40 platinum prints that were informed by these ideas. Before long, however, he became dissatisfied with rendering everything in sharp focus, considering that the undiscriminating emphasis it gave to all objects was unlike the way the human eye saw the world.

He then experimented with soft focus, but was unhappy with the results that this gave too, experiencing difficulty with accurately recreating the depth and atmosphere which he saw as necessary to capture nature with precision. Despite his misgivings, he took many photographs of landscapes and rural life in the East Anglian fenlands and published seven further books of his photography through the next ten years. In the last two of these volumes, *On*

English Lagoons (1893) and *Marsh Leaves* (1895), Emerson printed the photographs himself using photogravure, after having bad experiences with commercial printers.

After the publication of *Marsh Leaves* in 1895, generally considered to be his best work, Emerson published no further photographs, though he continued writing and publishing books, both works of fiction and on such varied subjects as genealogy and billiards. In 1924, he started writing a history of artistic photography and completed the manuscript just before his death in Falmouth, Cornwall on 12 May 1936.

In 1979 he was inducted into the International Photography Hall of Fame.

Maud Isabel Ebbutt

Maud Isabell Ebbutt (born 1867) was a British writer who published *Hero Myths & Legends of the British Race* in 1910. In her introduction she wrote that:.

"'Hero-worship endures forever while man endures,' wrote Thomas Carlyle, and this fidelity of men to their admiration for great heroes is one of the surest tokens by which we can judge of their own character. Such as the hero is, such will his worshippers be; and the men who idolised Robin Hood will be found to have been men who were themselves in revolt against oppressive law, or who, finding law powerless to prevent tyranny, glorified the lawless punishment of wrongs and the bold denunciation of perverted justice. The warriors who listened to the saga of Beowulf looked on physical prowess as the best of all heroic qualities, and the Normans who admired Roland saw in him the ideal of feudal loyalty. To every age, and to every nation, there is a peculiar ideal of heroism, and in the popular legends of each age this ideal may be found."

ABOUT THE EDITOR

I was born in 1962 into a predominantly sporting household – Dad being a good footballer, playing senior amateur and lower league professional football in England, as well as running a series of private businesses in partnership with mum, herself an accomplished and medal winning dancer.

I obtained a degree in History from Leeds University before wandering rather haphazardly into the emerging world of business computing in the late nineteen-eighties.

A little like my sporting father, I followed a succession of amateur writing paths alongside my career in technology, including working as a freelance journalist and book reviewer, my one claim to fame being a by-line in a national newspaper in the UK, The Sunday People.

I also spent 10 years treading the boards, appearing all over the south of the UK in pantos and plays, in village halls and occasionally on the stage of a professional theatre or two.

Following the sporting theme, and a while after I hung up my own boots, I worked on live TV broadcasts for the BBC, ITV, TVNZ, EuroSport and others as a rugby "Stato", covering Heineken Cups, Six Nations, IRB World Sevens and IRB World Cups in the late '90's and early '00's.

I try to combine my love of storytelling with a passion for information technology, and am currently Vice President - Technology with a major UK FinTech company.

You can find out more about me on the Bio page or at: www.boyonabench.com

 SOLITUDE

Lightning Source UK Ltd.
Milton Keynes UK
UKHW011241191120
373690UK00002B/364